FOOTBALL
HERO

FOO
HI

SCHOLASTIC INC.
New York Toronto London Auckland Sydney
Mexico City New Delhi Hong Kong Buenos Aires

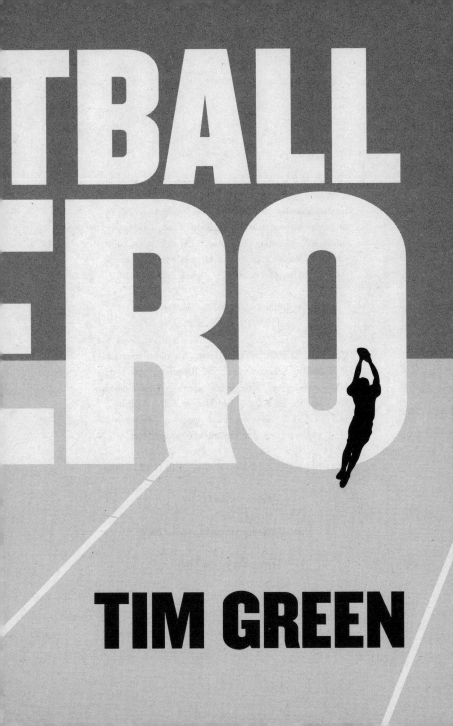

ISBN-13: 978-0-545-20295-4
ISBN-10: 0-545-20295-7

12 11 10 9 8 7 6 5 4 3 2 1   9 10 11 12 13 14/0

Printed in the U.S.A.   40

First Scholastic printing, September 2009

Typography by Joel Tippie

For my beautiful wife Illyssa,
and for Ty, the perfect gift at the perfect time

"The real glory is being knocked to your knees
and then coming back. That's real glory.
That's the essence of it."
—Vince Lombardi

CHAPTER ONE

TURNING TWELVE DIDN'T MATTER to Ty. Birthdays, like Christmas and every other holiday, had lost their thrill. Most of the day had already passed without anything special happening and Ty didn't expect that to change. He knew the surprise his aunt and uncle had promised him wouldn't amount to much more than a pair of underwear or a new ax for splitting wood, maybe a blanket. Surprises had a place in his other life, the one before his parents died.

But when Ty grabbed the handrail and stepped up into the school bus, he was surprised when someone yanked him back to earth and spun him around.

"Why weren't you in gym class?"

Coach V had a voice like a growling Doberman, and he scowled down at Ty without easing the stranglehold

1

on his upper arm. Ty's face overheated. He swallowed and looked around. The bus at the front of the line hissed and roared, grinding gears and filling the air with a cloud of diesel fumes.

"I was in Mrs. Brennan's office," Ty said, looking down at the broken line of the curb. Mrs. Brennan was the school psychologist.

The coach ran a hand over the bristles of his dark hair, and his face softened a bit.

"You're not in trouble?" he asked softly.

Ty looked at his blue no-name sneakers and shook his head. "For the accident."

"Does she help?" the coach asked, still soft.

Ty knew that when adults asked questions, they already had the answer they wanted in mind. The right answer wasn't that the death of his mom and dad had left a hole in his heart too big to be helped. The right answer was yes, and that's what he said.

Coach V nodded and turned his big, sharp nose in the direction of the bus, eyes hiding behind the kind of mirror sunglasses that cops usually wore, the kind that reminded Ty of a housefly.

"We got spring football today," the coach said, turning the insect eyes back at Ty so that he could see two dark-haired boys with glasses staring back in their mirrors. "You interested?"

"Spring football?" Ty asked, blinking and pushing his own glasses back up to the top of his nose.

"It's a club, just for one week," Coach V said. "It lets me get the team together to see where we're at. They didn't have spring football in your old school?"

"I went to Tully. There's no football until you get to high school."

"Small town, huh?"

Ty jumped when his bus driver blared her horn and bellowed out at him, "Let's go!"

"There's a sports bus at five," the coach said.

"You think I could play?" Ty asked.

The coach looked up at the bus driver with a twisted smile and pumped his thumb toward the exit.

"Go ahead, I got him," he said to the driver.

The door slammed shut, and the bus growled away, unleashing the long line of waiting buses to do the same. Ty couldn't hear the coach's words over their roar until they reached the top steps of the school.

"I'm sorry," Ty said. "I didn't hear you."

"Of course I want you to play," the coach said. "You're the fastest kid in sixth grade and I need some deep speed for my passing game."

"I'm not too skinny?" Ty said, glancing down at his thin legs.

"Deion Sanders was skinny, but if you're the fastest man on the planet it doesn't matter."

"Who's Deion Sanders?"

Coach V stopped and looked at him, then shook his head and said, "You're too young."

Ty swung the old pillowcase his aunt made him use for a book bag over his shoulder and hustled to keep up. "My older brother plays football."

"Great," the coach said. He swung open the locker room door and banged his palm on one of the old metal lockers. "Get your gym clothes on and get outside."

"At Syracuse," Ty said, setting his pillowcase full of books down on the scarred wooden bench.

Coach V froze and whipped off his sunglasses as he spun around.

"Not Tiger Lewis?"

"Uh-huh."

"*The* Tiger Lewis? That's your brother?"

"His real name is Thane. They just call him Tiger."

"How come you never said?"

Ty shrugged and searched for the right answer.

In truth, he kept his older brother a secret because he already got picked on enough for being the new kid at school. Picked on for reading all the time, his glasses, the musty pillowcase he used to carry his books, his canvas grocery-store sneakers, and his skinny legs. He imagined that if he claimed Tiger Lewis for his brother, the kids would either refuse to believe him or they would point out how pitiful he was compared to his all-American brother, the football hero.

In truth, it sometimes seemed to Ty that he only imagined Tiger Lewis was his brother. The two of them were so far apart in age—ten years—that they really didn't know each other that well. Ty had been eight when Thane went off to college. Since then, he only got to see his older brother on holidays or family vacations. Two weeks every summer their mom and dad used to take them camping, once in July, once in August. The memory of those times flashed in his mind, like dreams—being out in a small boat, just him and Thane, or climbing a rocky mountain trail, Thane reaching down to help him, the veins protruding from his muscular forearms.

When they were together, Thane, or Tiger, as everyone called him now, would share his knowledge with Ty. He'd tell stories with lessons and say that he wanted Ty to learn from the mistakes he'd already made. Thane's nuggets of wisdom would come back to Ty at random moments, crashing through his consciousness like a loud commercial in the middle of a television program. When they did, Ty would lose himself for a moment as if in a trance. One of those memories came back to him now.

He and Thane stood on the bare face of a massive rock atop Bald Mountain in the middle of the Adirondacks, waiting for their parents to catch up. Clouds floated by in their blue field. Lakes glittered below, gems nestled into the pine trees. A warm breeze cooled the sweat on their faces, and the scent of balsam floated by. They had been talking about a book Thane gave him where a boy raised by a witch got picked on. Thane said he knew what that boy felt like.

"No one ever picked on you," Ty had said.

"That what you think?" Thane asked him, squinting his eyes into the sun and pointing to a golden eagle.

"Look at you," Ty said. "You'd kill anyone who picked on you."

"Think again," Thane said, glancing at him. "I got like this lifting weights. I had legs skinnier than you, glasses, zits on my face, always reading books. Yeah, they got me. Dumped my books. Gum on my chair. All that."

"What happened?" Ty asked.

Thane shrugged and said, "Then I found the game."

"Football?"

"There's only one," Thane said.

"Hey," Coach V said, shaking Ty by the shoulder. "You okay?"

"Huh?" Ty said.

Coach V wrinkled his brow, raised one eyebrow, and pointed toward the door. "You do that on the field and you'll get your clock cleaned. Hurry up."

Coach V turned without waiting and banged open the locker room door, disappearing into the warm afternoon sunlight.

Ty flung open his locker and tore off his clothes. He

threw on his gym shirt and shorts, stiff and ripe from two-day-old dried sweat. One of the other things he remembered Thane telling him was to tie his shoes tight before any contest.

"Easy to remember," Thane said one day, before all the bad things happened. "That's your name. Don't forget to tie, Ty."

Ty put his left foot on the bench and bent over, pulling the laces snug and retying the sneaker so that it hugged his foot. He switched feet, but when he tugged on the ratty gray laces of his right shoe, one snapped off down at the eye hole. It would take several minutes to relace the sneaker. Ty began, but the whistle sounded outside and he sprang up and sprinted through the door with a loose shoe, exactly what his brother had warned him to never do.

CHAPTER TWO

THE TEAM WAS SPREAD out across the grass, spaced evenly in rows like chocolate candies in a box. Ty found a spot in the back and reached down to touch his toes with everybody else. Every time he began to work on his shoelace, Coach V started them doing a different stretch, until Ty simply gave up.

After stretching, Coach V barked out an order. The lines compressed to one side, and the team ran back and forth across the width of the field in waves. Agility drills. High stepping. Backpedaling. Shuffling. Crisscrossing. The whistle blew again, and Coach V shouted for quarterbacks and receivers to come with him, and for the linemen to go with Coach Full. Everyone seemed to know exactly what to do and exactly where to go. Ty did his best to follow along, slipping into the back of a line of receivers who began dashing down the field for ten yards before breaking in at a forty-five-degree angle, a post route, to catch a pass from one of the three quarterbacks.

Halpern Middle School had more than two thousand kids in three grades, and Ty had only been there since the winter break, so he knew only a few of the boys in his line. One he did recognize was Calvin West, a tall, broad-shouldered boy with blond hair that hung like a curtain around his tan face. Calvin told everyone he'd grown up in San Diego, on a surfers' beach. He wore a shark's tooth on a thin leather choker around his long neck. When Ty stepped up for his turn, Calvin recognized him from the back.

"Lewis!" he shouted, pointing toward the adjacent field and grinning at the other boys. "The girl's softball team is practicing over there."

Everyone laughed. Ty ignored them and crouched down into a stance, ready to run. The quarterback yelled, "Hike," and Ty took off, ten yards of blurred hands, feet, and long, thin legs. He gave a small head fake to the outside, as if some defensive back were covering him, then he broke to the inside the way the others had. Ty felt his foot leave the shoe and take off like a bird. The world tilted, then flipped, and he felt the heavy jolt of the ground popping his chin and chipping off the end of a tooth.

His ears burned at the sound of howling boys. He got up slow, brushing at the grass embedded now into the surface of his bare knees.

"What the heck was that?" Coach V asked, fighting back a smile.

"My shoe," Ty said.

"No-name tear-away specials," Calvin West said to a chorus of more hooting.

"All right," Coach V said, glowering at the boys, "cut the crap. Let's go. Next."

Ty staggered over to his shoe, scooping it up just in time for the next boy to flash past him, make the break, and catch the pass. Ty jogged to the back of the line and sat down to relace his shoe. He missed his turn but got the laces even and tugged them tight. This time the other side snapped off.

"Ty!" Coach V called from over where the quarterbacks stood. "You with us or not?"

Ty felt the pressure build up behind his face, and the ducts in the corners of his eyes began to work. But before anyone could laugh, he sniffed, jumped up, kicked off both shoes, tore off his socks, and lined up in a stance, ready to go. Coach V shook his head but nodded to Michael Poyer, the team's first-string quarterback, who hiked the ball. This time, Ty streaked forward, made the break, and looked for the ball, ready to catch it. The ball came late, though, way behind him.

"You gotta *really* lead him," Coach V said, barking at Poyer.

"I tried," Poyer said, shaking his head.

"Do it again," the coach said. "Ty?"

Ty nodded and jogged back to the front of the line. His feet tingled at the touch of the prickly grass between his bare toes. He ran the pattern with blazing speed; the ball came late again, high and fast, but this time only an arm's length behind him. Ty left his feet and spun. The sun's rays blinded him. His hands flashed out into space and felt the sting of the leather ball.

CHAPTER THREE

TY SNATCHED THE FOOTBALL from the air and hit the ground running up the field. He kept going until he reached the goal line, then slowed and jogged back.

"Wow," Poyer said, looking from Ty to Coach V.

"Wow is right," the coach said.

West stood silent with his arms folded across his chest until, in a low voice, he said, "Let's see how cute he looks with a free safety waiting to tear his head off."

Ty got into the back corner of the sports bus and split open his ragged paperback copy of *Watership Down*. He had plenty of time. His was the very last stop. Ty's aunt Virginia and uncle Gus didn't live in one of the big new houses with sprawling lawns that people thought of when they thought of Halpern.

Neither did they live in one of the dozens of renovated colonial houses clustered around the heart of the historic little village with its antique shops, fancy restaurants, pubs, and expensive clothing stores.

Aunt Virginia's house was little more than a trailer with a roof.

"Kid. Kid! Let's go, I got my bowling league."

Ty peered over the seat to see the bus driver's eyes glaring at him from the big rectangular mirror up front. He fumbled with the book, turned down the corner of the page, and slipped it into his pillowcase.

"Sorry," he said, jumping down the steps and onto the gravel shoulder of rural Highway 626. The bus hissed and pulled away as Ty started down the dirt track. Overhead, a robin sang from its perch on the electric pole. Ty rounded a bend, and the scrubby trees on either side of the track opened into a small grassy clearing. His aunt's house cowered at the back of the clearing, beneath a towering stand of thick pines.

Instead of climbing the stack of cinder blocks that served as the front step, Ty skirted around the house and down a small dirt trail that disappeared into the pines. He needed to use the bathroom, and Ty wasn't allowed to use the one in the house. Forty feet inside the tree line, the path ended at a bright blue Porta Potti. Ty took a deep breath and pulled open the door, hoping to finish his business before he had to take another breath and failing as he always did.

Not long after Ty had arrived in Halpern, Uncle Gus found the broken Porta Potti at a dump just outside Newark. Ty spent an entire Saturday digging the five-foot-deep hole. Then he helped Uncle Gus roll the bright blue plastic capsule off the back of his truck and out into the pines, where they set it up over the top of the pit. It wasn't so bad to go out into the woods, especially since the weather had warmed up, and Ty really understood. His aunt and uncle hadn't been looking to have a twelve-year-old boy dumped on them, and they deserved the privacy of their own bathroom. They already had to share it with their quiet and quirky teenage daughter, Charlotte, who took hour-long baths that outraged Uncle Gus, which prompted Aunt Virginia to snap at him like a lioness protecting her cub.

Ty trudged back to the house, past the woodpiles, and in the side door, where he washed his hands in the laundry room. Along the wall rested a stale mattress that Uncle Gus called a perfectly good bed. At night, Ty would tip it down onto the faded particleboard floor. The walls boasted bare two-by-four studs trimmed with electric wire, pipes, and an open vent that sometimes leaked heat into the otherwise chilly little space.

When he shut off the water and the pipes stopped their groaning, his aunt's voice pierced his eardrums.

"Ty!" she screamed.

Ty snatched a damp towel from the floor and dashed into the kitchen.

"I didn't hear you, Aunt Virginia," he said, drying his fingers. "I was washing my hands."

His aunt kept her long, straight hair tucked behind her ears, and it made the big round glasses she wore seem like the bottoms of two soup cans, each with a single black bullet hole punched in its center to serve as an eye. Two overgrown eyebrows—thick like woolly-bear caterpillars—dropped scowling toward the bridge of her long, narrow nose. Her lips, pale as rain-soaked worms, stretched tight across her big teeth.

"Where were you?" she said, her words trembling with rage.

"Spring football practice, Aunt Virginia," Ty said.

"Today's your *birth*day," she said.

"So I thought you wouldn't mind."

"So I thought you wouldn't mind," she said, mimicking him with a high-pitched song, tilting her head from side to side before she frowned again. "You were told that we had a surprise for you when you got home. Did you forget? Are you *that* stupid?"

Ty didn't answer. His eyes lost focus as he drifted back to an earlier time.

A little bald man shook his fist at Tiger for taking his parking spot. The two of them had driven their

*dad's Subaru from their campsite to the grocery store
in Racquette Lake to pick up the marshmallows he'd
forgotten to pack.*

*"Why didn't you smash that guy's face?" Ty asked,
hurrying after Tiger into the store. "Or cuss him out
anyway? You were there first."*

*Tiger snatched a bag of marshmallows from the
shelf, smiled at him, and said, "It doesn't matter what
someone else thinks of you or what they say about you.
You have to know what you are, who you are. That's
what matters. A guy like that, just pretend every time
he opens his mouth that it's a fart. That's all it is
anyway."*

Ty grinned.

"What in the *world* do you think is so funny?" Aunt
Virginia asked, the color of her face showing hints of
purple.

CHAPTER FOUR

AUNT VIRGINIA LEANED TOWARD Ty so that he could smell the remains of the tuna sandwich she'd eaten for lunch.

"I, uh, I was thinking about something else, Aunt Virginia," Ty said.

"Don't you go into one of your trances on *me*," she said. "Save those shenanigans for Mrs. Brennan. Your *uncle* will be back soon and he is not happy. You can just chop wood until he gets here."

Ty knew better than to ask for something to eat, even on his birthday. He knew he'd be fed sooner or later, just not when he wanted and certainly not if he asked. Part of the reason he didn't feel so bad about the way his aunt treated him was because Charlotte would occasionally get a taste of it herself. For every minute Aunt Virginia spent crooning over Charlotte's pink nail polish or braiding her scraggly blond hair, she'd spend another minute grouching at her about wiping her feet or getting a C in math.

So Ty didn't take it personal. Even though Aunt Virginia had been his father's sister, he figured that deep down, kids rubbed her the wrong way. She also found it hard to pretend that they didn't get on her nerves. If nothing else, she was honest.

The other consolation was that Ty's father had apparently gotten Aunt Virginia's share of familial affection. Ty had enjoyed over eleven years of kisses, hugs, and regular praise from both his parents. So, when he calculated it out, even spending the next six years with Aunt Virginia and Uncle Gus would leave him well ahead of many kids.

Ty returned to Uncle Gus's mountain of wood, pulling thick logs off the pile, splitting them with the dull ax, and placing their splintered parts neatly onto the stacks. From the top of a pine tree, a song sparrow trilled, then cocked its head to watch. Dizzy from the work, Ty set a fresh stick of wood on the chopping block and let his arms fall to his side. Small storms of insects swirled in the light that glinted at him through the trees. Ty turned his face into the small breeze to dry his sweat and heard the broken rumble of Uncle Gus's black F 150 with the big white cover on the back.

When he opened his eyes, Uncle Gus's face glowered at him through the tint of the cracked windshield. Beside him, Charlotte's face glowed like a small moon, her features as expressionless as the craters on the dead planet. Ty raised the ax, half as a salute, half to prove that he'd been at work. His uncle slid down from the truck and marched toward Ty with a big round belly and a bowlegged stride.

Uncle Gus's hair had already begun to gray, but it was thick as a rug and only stayed brushed over to the side with help from a tin of greasy pomade. A matching walrus mustache covered most of his mouth. The corners of his milky green eyes, like the mustache and the rolls of fat in his neck, drooped toward the ground. His business, a cleaning service, had left his stumpy strong hands chapped, red, and hard as granite.

He pointed a stout cherry finger at Ty as he approached and Ty's stomach sank. From the corner of his eye, Ty saw Aunt Virginia pop out of the washroom door and stand with her arms folded across her chest like an angry spectator. From the truck, Charlotte gave him a sympathetic look before she ducked down behind the dashboard, pretending to adjust the radio.

"You," Uncle Gus said, his voice and finger trembling together. "You slacker. Lazy. Tricky. Lying."

Uncle Gus's eyes were set close together, sometimes

making him appear to be cross-eyed, especially when he was mad. His face expanded, turning colors before he let the air out, hissing like a busted radiator from beneath his mustache.

"*He* went to football practice," Aunt Virginia said in her singsong mimic.

"Football?" Uncle Gus said, stopping in his tracks, his dark eyebrows wrinkling. "It's your birthday. You're *twelve*."

"That's why I thought you wouldn't mind."

Uncle Gus shot an accusing look at Aunt Virginia. He would often complain to her, out of the blue, that she spoiled Ty and no good would come from it.

Uncle Gus snapped his fingers at his wife before holding his hand out, palm up. From her apron she produced a rolled-up document tied with a bit of red yarn in a knot, so that the ends hung limp without the fanfare of a bow. Uncle Gus's fingers curled around the paper tube. He slowly swung his arm toward Ty before he opened his fingers again.

"Work is a privilege," he said in a whisper. "You need to learn that. Happy birthday, boy."

Uncle Gus jiggled his hand until Ty reached out and took his surprise. He slipped the yarn off the end of the tube and unrolled it to find an official state document, the paper thick and coarse to the touch, the ink letters fat and fancy. Ty's heart pattered as he read, thinking the certificate might have some connection to his parents and would somehow hold the key to his freedom. Maybe it was a bond or some hidden cache of wealth that would pay for college.

But as his stomach settled and he began to decipher the words, his daydream turned into a nightmare.

CHAPTER FIVE

TY'S BIRTHDAY SURPRISE WAS a work permit from the state of New Jersey.

"Most kids can't work until sixteen," Uncle Gus said with a nod. "'Cept if it's a family business. Which this is."

Uncle Gus nodded toward the truck and Charlotte's impassive face. On the side of the rusty black F 150 was a plastic sign with red letters that said: "Slatz's Cleaning Services, Proprietor: Gus Slatz."

"Coach V wants me to play wide receiver," Ty heard himself say. "He thinks I'm the fastest kid in my class."

Uncle Gus smiled, glancing at his wife as if Ty were telling a joke.

"Fast enough for him to give you a big fat contract

like your brother's gonna get?" Uncle Gus said. "They gonna pay you, you're so good?"

Ty opened his mouth, but nothing came out.

"No, they ain't," Uncle Gus said, then he poked one of those stubby red fingers into Ty's chest. "You got to make money in this world, boy. No time for games. You ain't no football player. You ain't Tiger and your daddy didn't leave you no insurance money when he ran his car off that road. He didn't leave you with nothin' but us. That's it. Now, I could be bitter about that, my wife's brother just dumpin' his kid on me when I got my own already, but I'm not like that. I'm bigger than that, the churchgoing type.

"Give a man a fish, feed him for a day," Uncle Gus said, glancing at his wife with a knowing look and taking on the aspect of a preacher. "But teach a man to fish, you feed him for a lifetime. I'm gonna teach you to fish. Teach you to work."

Ty looked at the mountain of wood and the three long, tall rows he'd split and stacked over the previous months.

Uncle Gus grinned and winked at the woodpile, then he shook his head. "See? You think *that* was work. You got no idea, but I'm gonna show you work. Every day. You get right home after school. Four till midnight, you'll get a full day's work. Happy birthday, boy.

"Now, get your scrawny butt in the truck."

According to Uncle Gus, the ride to Lucy's Bar took

twice as long because they had to go back home and pick up Ty and now they were caught in traffic. He complained about that the whole way, smoking cigarette after cigarette. Ty's eyes watered from the smoke. When he reached over to roll down the window, his uncle slapped at his hand and told him to leave it up.

"You trying to give Charlotte an allergy attack?" Uncle Gus asked, scowling so that the vein in the middle of his forehead bulged.

Charlotte popped her gum and stared straight ahead without saying a thing. Her dirty wheat-colored hair hung limp and straight and long, parted in the middle to expose a scalp line as pale as the skin on her face and her bony arms. Sometimes, she reminded Ty of a horror movie victim, with her hunched narrow shoulders and vacant milky green eyes big as jumbo marbles.

But the simple curves of her round face and the faded pink polish on her nails suggested something more pleasant might be hidden within. And, although she'd never said anything particularly nice to Ty, neither had she ever said anything particularly mean. In Ty's lonely world, he considered her to be on the friendly side of the ledger.

Eventually, they did get there, pulling off the highway onto a broken service road littered with low, grimy buildings. The telephone wires hung slack between their poles as if exhausted, unadorned by birds of any kind. This close to the tidal swamps of Secaucus, the hazy air owned a funk that made Ty wrinkle his nose as he climbed out of the truck. They entered Lucy's Bar through the back.

Uncle Gus left the two of them with the buckets, mops, brooms, vacuum, and cleaning supplies in a little hallway and disappeared into the front. Ty peered into a tiny kitchen where a man as big as a bear, wearing a full beard and a backward Jets cap, smoked a cigarette while laying circles of dough into a vat of boiling grease. On his massive bare arm, swirling snake tattoos surrounded the name "MIKE." Ty sniffed at the scent of donuts mixed with stale bread and hamburger meat gone bad.

Mike turned his head and squinted at Ty through the smoke. Ty felt dizzy.

Ty and Thane walked out of the Old Forge theater into the night. When they turned the corner to where their car was parked, they startled a crooked old man picking through the garbage. In his hand was a half-eaten chicken leg smeared with ketchup that he quickly concealed behind his back, licking his lips. He blinked at them and sniffed and stepped sideways off the curb to make room so they could pass.

Thane dug into his pockets, removing their change from the movie and holding it out for the startled old man.

"I think you dropped this," Thane said, waiting for

the man to hold out his hand. When he did, Thane let the money fall. He took Ty by the arm and led him away.

Ty glanced over his shoulder. "Why'd you do that? That was for ice cream. That guy was a bum."

"What if he wasn't?" Thane asked.

Ty wrinkled his brow and said, "What do you mean?"

"Don't judge someone by what you see," Thane said. "I met this bum once who was a doctor. His wife died and he kind of lost his marbles. Sometimes people just run out of luck and they start to look like something they're not. Don't get me wrong, sometimes they're exactly what they look like, but you always have to wait to find out. It's what's inside that counts.

"Don't judge a book by its cover."

From the pocket of his enormous jeans, the cook removed a switchblade knife, flicking it open and turning the point so that it glinted at Ty. Mike's grin proved to be missing the front teeth. On the knuckles of his hand were the letters "K-I-L-L." Ty stepped back, bumping into Charlotte, who shoved him so that he tripped and stumbled halfway into the tiny kitchen.

CHAPTER SIX

INSTEAD OF IMPALING TY, the colossal cook dipped his blade into the boiling vat and removed two golden brown miniature donuts. He let them slide from the knife into a paper bag, which he shook, producing little puffs of white smoke. Then the knife went back into the bag and Mike held the powdery donuts out for Ty with a grunt, nodding his head until Ty removed them and handed one to Charlotte.

"Thanks," Ty said. He took a small bite, then devoured the rest, the dough and sugar melting together into his watering mouth.

The door at the end of the little hallway banged open, and Uncle Gus reappeared, wiping his bushy gray mustache on a sleeve. Uncle Gus's watery eyes left Ty thinking that he'd had a drink. He had the look of a Saturday afternoon when he'd sit watching ball games in his chair, drinking beer after beer. Uncle Gus glared as Ty licked clean the remaining powder from his lips.

"Hey," Mike said in a loud rumble from the kitchen. "Gus."

Uncle Gus's scowl brightened instantly at the sign of Mike. He stepped into the kitchen and looked up at the cook, wringing his hands and telling him how much it meant to the kids that he would give them a snack.

"It's not every day a middle-school kid gets a donut made by a former NFL lineman," Uncle Gus said.

"Wait there," Mike said in a deep, rumbling voice. He stuck the cigarette into the corner of his mouth and turned to his stove.

Uncle Gus spun around at Ty and made sneering faces while Mike removed another donut from the vat. Ty looked past his uncle to see the big man stick a finger into his nose and remove a bloody booger with a half-inch tail of quavering snot. Mike winked at Ty, then smeared the mess onto the donut before popping it into the bag of sugar. Ty curled his lower lip into his mouth and clamped down hard.

"You think something is funny?" Uncle Gus asked, his face going red.

Uncle Gus calmed down, though, when Mike nudged him and removed the donut from the bag with his switchblade. Uncle Gus took it, forcing a smile, and Mike sucked on his cigarette. Mike gave a thumbs-up and squinted at Uncle Gus until he popped the entire donut into his mouth, chewing so that his big mustache danced up and down on his face. Mike smiled and nodded, laughing so deep that the cigarette tumbled from his lips and Uncle Gus joined him. Ty stole a look at Charlotte's blank face and thought he saw a twinkle in her eye. Laughter burst from him, and Uncle Gus looked at him uncertainly, swallowing in the nick of time. Mike walloped him so hard on the back that Uncle Gus stumbled out into the hallway.

"Well," Uncle Gus said, grinning up at the ex-player, "back to work. That was delicious."

"I bet it was," Mike said.

Uncle Gus turned on Ty and Charlotte, flicked his fingers to shoo them down the hall, and said, "Hurry up."

"He's big," Ty said in a low voice.

"Six-seven, four hundred pounds these days," Uncle Gus said. "Seventh-round draft pick by the Giants in 1986. Blew out his knee halfway through his rookie season, put a hundred pounds on during rehab, and never got back onto the field. Let's go."

Uncle Gus jumped ahead of them and held open the swinging door, waving them into the main bar.

Ty and Charlotte carried in the equipment and

supplies. Lucy's was a dingy place with battered wooden chairs and tables carved with graffiti. It smelled of stale beer, and Ty's sneakers made sticky sucking noises as he walked.

"That's Lucy," Uncle Gus said, nodding toward the front window, where a tired row of men, their backs to the glass, sat hunched over their drinks. One sat apart from the rest like a shepherd guarding his flock. "You don't even try to talk to him. Be careful of the bar if you ever clean over there. Don't bang your mop into it. His father made it. And, if he catches you looking at the burn mark on his face, you'll have a couple burn marks of your own. Get it?"

"Lucy? He's a man," Ty said without thinking.

"And *not* a nice man," his uncle said.

Uncle Gus pointed to the back and said, "You see that red door next to the bathrooms? That door's closed, you don't touch it. If it's open, you go in there and clean the bathroom and empty the trash. Don't *touch* anything else. That's Lucy's office. The bar, the office, and his scar, just be careful with all of it."

At the corner of the bar the man named Lucy sat with a bottle of beer, a newspaper, and a bowl of peanuts.

"What's that thing next to the peanuts?" Ty asked.

Uncle Gus glanced Lucy's way and said, "A crowbar. I've seen him use it, too."

Lucy wore the shadow of a beard and the hungry

face of someone who hadn't eaten for days. Ty presumed the shiny red lozenge in the middle of his sunken cheek was the burn. With one hand, Lucy snapped open the peanuts, popping them into his mouth and slowly grinding them down before adding their shells to the mess on the floor. With his other hand, he worked a cell phone, talking, dialing, and text messaging nonstop. He kept his eyes glued to the TV above the bar, where a Mets game played without sound.

Uncle Gus pointed to the vacuum and told Charlotte to get going. She carried the machine over to the thin carpeted area where a dozen tables sat between two rows of booths. Charlotte plugged the vacuum into the wall and got right to it, filling the room with a whir so loud Ty had to lean closer to his uncle to hear.

"I said start with the bathrooms," Uncle Gus said, nudging a bucket with his toe and rattling the contents—a toilet brush, a mop, a sponge, and a bottle of ammonia.

Ty picked up the bucket and headed for the far wall, where the men's and women's rooms stood side by side, each with several holes punched into it. Before going in, he glanced back to see his uncle sweeping up the pile of peanut shells beneath Lucy's stool. His uncle glanced up and made a snarling face and Ty ducked inside.

The smell made him retch. A reddish brown spray of vomit coated the tiled wall above the urinal. The floor was yellow and sticky. Inside the stall, the bowl had been jammed with a mound of soggy paper and crap. Ty uncapped the ammonia and spilled it into the bucket, wincing as the acrid smell burned his eyes.

The bucket wouldn't fit into the sink.

He looked around for a spigot he could use to fill it with water but found nothing more than filth smeared across the walls. After several minutes, he returned to the bar, where the peanut shells had disappeared. His uncle now sat beside Lucy, bent over a mug of beer and pointing to something in the newspaper.

"I don't care what that says," the wiry owner said, punching a text message into his phone. "The spread's three, take it or leave it."

Ty cleared his throat and the men spun around. Lucy glared and crushed a peanut in his fist.

CHAPTER SEVEN

TY STARED AT HIS sneakers, determined not to look at Lucy's scar.

"Big birthday boy. See what I said about this kid?" Uncle Gus said, banging his mug on the bar.

"Didn't get his brother's legs, I tell you that," said Lucy, flicking a peanut shell so that it bounced off Ty's chest.

"I don't know where to fill the bucket," Ty said quietly. He glanced at the row of men who sat gripping their drinks. They stared at him with dead eyes and mouths that hung slack.

"What do you think that hose is for?" Uncle Gus asked.

"I didn't see a hose," Ty said, daring a look at his uncle. "And the toilet's clogged, too."

Lucy snorted and slid down off his chair, rounding the bar and returning with a plunger that he held out in front of Ty until he took it.

"Check in the other bucket for the hose," Uncle Gus said, "and get going. We're behind."

"He the reason you're late?" Lucy said, snorting again. He picked the crowbar up off the bar and poked it in Ty's direction. One end of the blue metal tool flattened into a wedge while the other hooked into a claw.

"Thought he'd stay after school," Uncle Gus said. "Spring football. Thinks he's his brother."

Lucy chuckled. His phone rang and he flipped it open and said hello, replacing the crowbar and turning his back on them. Uncle Gus gripped Ty's shoulder until he looked up. Uncle Gus made his eyes really wide and jerked his head in the direction of the bathrooms.

Ty found the piece of hose in the other bucket. He used the mixture of ammonia and water to mop the floors and the walls, and he plunged out the toilet, stopping several times to gag. The women's room was worse.

As he finished, the door was flung open, and Uncle Gus looked around.

"Not a bad job," he said, bending over the sink and touching the faucet with his fingertip. "I didn't even know these faucets were silver, but you're way too slow. Let's go."

On their way to the next account, a small office building, Ty learned from his uncle that Slatz's Cleaning Services served a variety of customers, including a car dealership, a donut shop, and a dentist's office. Each of them had bathrooms that needed cleaning, and that responsibility would fall to Ty. The bathrooms in the office building weren't nearly as dirty as the ones in Lucy's Bar, but Ty also got his fill of vacuuming, sweeping, cleaning windows, and emptying garbage.

It was nine o'clock by the time they finished the office building and their supplies were loaded back into the covered bed of the truck. When they climbed into the front, Ty's stomach rumbled loud enough to make Uncle Gus laugh.

"Don't worry," he said. "Next stop's the donut shop."

Ty glanced over at Charlotte, and even she moistened her lips in anticipation. When they arrived, Uncle Gus went straight to the garbage and pulled out a bag of day-old rolls.

"Perfectly good," he said, setting them out on a countertop and halving them with a sharp knife he took down off the wall. From the refrigerator, he removed wrapped slices of ham and a stack of cheese and laid them onto the rolls before sticking them into the microwave to cook. Ty sat next to Charlotte at the counter, his mouth watering while the appliance whirred away the seconds. When his uncle handed him the sandwich, the first bite burned his mouth, so he pulled the sandwich apart, allowing the steam to curl up out of the sticky cheese and blowing hard before putting it back together and wolfing it down in three bites.

When Uncle Gus's cell phone rang, he checked the number and licked his fingers deliberately before answering.

"Hello, Tiger," Uncle Gus said, his eyes gleaming at Ty. "Yes, the birthday boy is right here, having a little birthday dinner. Glad you didn't forget . . . Oh? An agent, huh? I hope he took you to a nice place. Those agents are rolling in it . . . Yeah, you too. Here's Ty."

Uncle Gus covered the phone and hissed at Ty. "We're one big *happy* family, right?"

Charlotte glanced at him, and Ty clamped his mouth shut, nodding yes until his uncle handed him the phone.

"Hey, Killer," Thane said. "Happy birthday. You doing all right?"

"Sure," Ty said.

"Got a surprise for you," Thane said. "Kind of a birthday present."

"Okay," Ty said, clenching his free hand.

"ESPN asked me down to New York for draft day. Everyone's starting to talk about me being a top five pick. The whole thing will be on TV. It's this Sunday."

"That's great."

"They said I could bring a guest. That's you."

"Me?" Ty asked, his heart doing loops.

"I land Saturday night at six. They've got a limo picking me up and then we'll come get you and spend the night in the Palace Hotel, some fancy place. It'll be you and me, just like old times. For a day anyway. Sound good?"

"I . . ." Ty said, his mind spinning. Uncle Gus gave him a crooked smile. "I got to ask Aunt Virginia and Uncle Gus."

"You don't think they'll let you?" Tiger asked.

"I don't know."

"Well, put Uncle Gus on," Tiger said. "Let's see what he says."

CHAPTER EIGHT

TY HANDED HIS UNCLE the phone.

Uncle Gus smiled at him and waggled his finger at the broom before pointing to the floor over by the entrance to the shop. Then he pointed at Charlotte and motioned with his thumb for her to get started in the kitchen. Charlotte rose from her seat without expression and floated past them, bending to scoop up a bucket of supplies without slowing down. Ty gripped the wooden handle of his broom and walked away, listening. When he glanced over his shoulder, he saw that Uncle Gus had turned away and was now hunched over the phone, muttering something to Thane.

Ty strained his ears, gently flicking the dust and dirt on the floor into a pile. He heard words like "in his best interest" and "church seems to be helping so much" and "wouldn't want to set him back." He knew instinctively that Uncle Gus was lying about him, but he couldn't think of what to do. When Uncle Gus said good-bye, Ty doubled his sweeping efforts and concentrated hard on the pile he'd created, ignoring the sound of his uncle's footsteps as best he could. He heard his uncle go to the glass case behind the counter and pick out a donut before he ambled toward Ty.

When Uncle Gus cleared his throat, Ty pretended to be surprised at his sudden presence.

"Oh, Uncle Gus," Ty said. "Can I say good-bye to Thane?"

"I said good-bye for you."

"What did he want?" Ty asked, trying to sound innocent.

Uncle Gus poked the rest of a jelly donut into his mouth and licked away the spot of powder still clinging to his finger.

"Brotherly love," Uncle Gus said through the mash of his donut. "Wants to spend a little time with you this weekend. Some ESPN thing, the draft and all that."

"Oh," Ty said, staring hopefully.

Uncle Gus swallowed and folded his arms across the belly of his pear-shaped torso.

"So, can I?" Ty asked.

"Well, that depends, doesn't it?" Uncle Gus said, stroking his thick mustache now and working a little blob of jelly into its bristles. "On how you're doing. Your attitude. Let's see how work goes. That's a good way to measure."

"Okay."

"Your brother is about to become a very rich man," Uncle Gus said.

"Oh."

"But he's not your guardian," Uncle Gus said. "I am. I'm the one with the grocery bills. I'm the one who has to be responsible."

"I know that, Uncle Gus," Ty said apologetically.

Uncle Gus pointed to a spot on the floor where someone had left a small wad of gum. "Pick that up."

As Ty bent down to do it, Uncle Gus walked away whistling.

In gym class the next day, Ty stifled a yawn and followed Coach V into his office while the rest of his classmates played dodgeball on the other side of the glass. Their hooting and hollering muscled its way through the walls, making the small, square office feel like an underwater chamber. The air was crowded with the smell of damp socks and basketballs.

Coach V sat in the squeaky chair, slid open his desk drawer, and removed a stapled stack of papers that he handed to Ty.

"Our playbook," the coach said, clapping his hands on the big hairy legs protruding from his shorts.

Ty squinted at the Xs and Os and the arrows and nodded. He'd seen Thane draw similar things on the backs of napkins for their father, explaining secret plays they would run against upcoming rivals, plays that put the ball into Thane's hands.

"Next fall," Coach V said, "you're gonna be my Z."

"Z?"

"Strong-side wide receiver," Coach V said, pointing to a single O on the very edge of the first page, the player farthest removed from all the others, the player with a long arrow sprouting from him like a spear. "That's our 'go' route. You just go, run as fast and as far as you can, and the quarterback heaves it up for you. With your speed, we could go, go, go. I'll show you out there today. After what I saw yesterday, I'm penciling you into the starting lineup. What do you think of that?"

"Coach."

"Some of your teammates aren't going to like it, but they'll get over it."

"Coach."

"Winning is like deodorant. I think John Madden said that. Something like that."

"Coach."

"What, Lewis?"

"I can't," Ty said, placing the stack of plays gently onto the desk.

"Don't worry about experience, it's speed. The

game is about speed. Don't say you can't do it. Trust me, you can."

"I mean, I can't play at all. I have to work. Every day. Right after school. Right when practice is."

Ty explained Slatz's Cleaning Services. Coach V sat with his mouth open, fishlike, and blinking.

"I got a work permit," Ty said after a few moments of nothing more than the sounds of screaming kids on the other side of the glass.

Coach V cleared his throat and slapped his knees before he rose. He sniffed as if he'd been insulted. "Well, if you can't play, you can't."

On his way to the door, Coach V put his hand on Ty's head, then let his grip slide down the back of Ty's neck, where he let go after a firm squeeze.

Ty followed the coach back out into the gym, where sneakers squeaked among the battle cries. Instead of joining the ruckus, Ty put his back to the padded wall behind the backboard and let himself slip down the wall until he sat planted on the wood floor with his head in his knees. He closed his eyes and forced himself to think about Saturday night and the one thing Uncle Gus hadn't yet said no to.

All he had to do was work hard. That's what he thought.

CHAPTER NINE

FRIDAY AFTER SCHOOL, UNCLE Gus sent Ty and Charlotte into the Breakfast Nook alone so he could listen to a Yankees/Red Sox game on the truck radio. They left him there, teeth grinding, hands clamped to the wheel, as Manny Ramirez stepped up to the plate.

The Nook, as they called it, was a small restaurant in a shopping center, an easy job to start out with, but farther away than the other accounts, and that's why Uncle Gus liked to get it done first, before they went to Lucy's Bar. The Nook only had one bathroom and apparently a very neat cook. The small kitchen rarely had anything more than some spattered pancake batter to worry about.

Ty mopped the kitchen floor, then went to work on the bathroom. He had given the toilet a final flush when he heard Charlotte squeal. He bolted back into the kitchen. A knife clattered to the bottom of the sink, and she cradled one hand in the other, stamping around the kitchen, crying.

"I'm bleeding," she said.

"Oh gosh," Ty said. "Hang on."

He yanked several paper towels off the roll on the wall and handed them to her. She plastered them to the long red gash across her palm, and the blood bloomed like a rose in a science movie. Charlotte sucked air in through her teeth with a hissing sound that reminded Ty of filling his bicycle tires at the gas station.

"You gotta hold it real tight," Ty said, clamping his own hands over hers and squeezing as well.

After a minute her breathing slowed.

"I think it stopped," she said quietly.

"Let's see," Ty said. He removed his hands and gently pulled the paper towel back. The angry red gash had begun to clot.

"Okay," he said, "but keep holding it for a while."

"What are you, a Boy Scout?" she asked. "You got a first aid badge or something?"

Ty felt his cheeks flush. "No. Thane—you know, my brother—he used to teach me all kinds of stuff like that. He's a lot older."

"Must be nice having a brother," she said, looking down at her hand.

"Should I get your dad?" he asked.

Charlotte glared up at him and shook her head.

"You might need stitches," Ty said, peering at her hand until she snatched it away and put it behind her back.

She looked scared, with her blue eyes wide open and her small red mouth making an O that reminded him of the playbook. Her blond hair had been pulled into the folds of a blue bandanna, making her face seem even rounder. It startled him to recognize something in her eyes, the same empty sadness that he saw in his own face when he looked into the bathroom mirror in school.

"Maybe I should get him," Ty said.

"Not when he's listening to a game. Never," she said. "It'll stop bleeding."

"It's just a game."

She puckered her mouth like she'd tasted something sour. "Not when you bet money it's not. When he does that, you don't want to be around. Especially if they lose. Did you ever know a gambler?"

Ty shook his head.

"Well, you do now. Welcome to the club. Can you finish the sink?" she asked in the soft voice of an ordinary girl.

Ty nodded and went to work, glancing back only when he heard the sound of the vacuum cleaner that she operated one-handed. Her face had returned to normal, lifeless as a loaf of bread. She turned the vacuum off at the same time he finished the sink. When he smiled at her and said he'd fill the napkin dispensers, only her eyes flickered at him. Besides that small glimmer and the bloodstained towel, Ty would have thought he'd imagined their entire conversation.

The minute Ty finished stuffing the last napkin holder, the front door crashed open, ringing the little bell so violently that it choked.

"Not done yet?" Uncle Gus screamed. His pasty face shone red, glazed with sweat. His eyes watered, and his teeth, like his fists, were clenched beneath the bushy mustache. "You two can't do anything without me, can you? You might as well be on the Yankees. Losers, all of you."

"I just finished, Uncle Gus," Ty said. "We can go."

Charlotte tossed her dust rag into a bucket and picked it up along with the vacuum, making for the door without a word. Uncle Gus pushed past her and walked into the kitchen. That's when he roared Ty's name.

"You call this clean?" he shouted.

Ty stepped into the doorway to see Uncle Gus stabbing his finger at the floor where three nickel-sized spots of blood glistened up at them.

Uncle Gus's face burned with rage.

CHAPTER TEN

"MOP THE FLOOR," UNCLE Gus said, growling. "I told you, first thing you do, and you didn't do it. What else didn't you do? AROD misses a grounder, the Yankees lose! You miss the floor, I lose the account! Get it? That's life. Just like you *not* going with your brother tomorrow night.

"That's life, too."

Ty felt his face fall. He clasped his hands.

"Don't look at me like that," Uncle Gus said. "We had a deal. You didn't live up to your end. I guess you didn't really want to go with him that bad after all."

Ty sat cringing in the middle seat. Uncle Gus cursed and smoked as he raced through traffic, passing people, leaning on his horn, and using his middle finger, on their way to the next job. To emphasize just how bad the Yankees played, he would wave his cigarette in the air, sending worms of ash tumbling about. Twice, the orange ember came close enough to Ty's face for him to feel its warmth.

When they got to Lucy's, Ty jumped out of the truck and headed past the empty kitchen and straight for the men's room. He held his breath as long as he could, mixing some ammonia into the bucket with water from his length of hose. Even through the battered door, Lucy's shouting made him jump. Slowly, he cracked open the door to see the action. Uncle Gus stood in front of the bar owner, wringing a dirty towel with his head hanging low. As much yelling as Uncle Gus could give out was about as much as he was now getting back from Lucy.

Lucy's eyes bulged, and he slapped the crowbar into the palm of his hand.

"Do I look like a bank?" Lucy yelled. "You know what happens to people who don't pay?"

Lucy raised the crowbar and Uncle Gus cringed. As angry as Ty had been in the truck ride over, he now felt terrible for his uncle, cowering like a puppy. Over in the eating area, Charlotte flipped on the vacuum and went to work on the carpet without seeming to pay attention. Ty eased the door shut and went to work. Not until he was finishing up with the toilet did the shouting subside. He heard Lucy go into the office on the other side of the wall and slam the door.

The toilet brush slipped from Ty's hand and clattered down into the corner of the stall. As Ty bent to pick it up, his ear brushed the rusty vent near the floor. That's when he heard the faint echo of a voice. Ty glanced over his shoulder, then touched his ear to the grate to hear Lucy talking on the phone to someone about a delivery of beer. Being able to hear the bar owner without his knowing sent a chill of danger up Ty's spine.

When the bathroom door suddenly swung open, Ty jumped. A shadow fell across him and he peered out from the stall.

"Can I get in there?"

Above him loomed Mike, the cook, all six foot seven, four hundred pounds of him. Ty pushed his glasses up on his nose, swallowed, and nodded, then glanced at the door.

"Don't worry about your uncle," the big man rumbled through his big dark beard. "They do this every couple weeks. Every time your uncle bets big, he loses big. Lucy won't really hurt him. He just talks like that."

Ty squeezed past Mike and reached for the doorknob. As he did, he noticed the backpack slung over the big man's shoulder and he wondered what it contained and why Mike would bring it into the bathroom with him.

"I used to have to go down the street to the Subway to use the bathroom," Mike said, wedging himself into the stall, closing the door, and dumping his backpack before letting his belt buckle clank to the floor with his pants. "Your uncle, he thinks throwing a bucket of ammonia in here and slamming the door is cleaning."

Ty didn't know how to respond. Should he thank the big man? Or tell him he wanted to do more with his life than cleaning toilets? He ended up saying nothing.

"You like that booger trick with your uncle?" Mike asked, his voice echoing off the tiled walls.

Ty froze. "You didn't do that to me, did you?"

The stall was silent for a moment before Mike sighed and said, "Your uncle's a horse's backside. I saw him giving you crap for having a donut and it ticked me off. A kid can't have a donut without catching grief?"

Ty breathed easier. "I laughed."

"I'll get him again with some earwax on your way out. Watch. Hey, don't stay here on account of me," Mike said. "It's about to get pretty bad."

Ty ducked out and saw his uncle sitting at the bar with his head in his hands. When Ty came out from cleaning the women's room, Uncle Gus was still there, but now Lucy had rejoined him. As if on cue, the two of them swung their heads around to look at him. Uncle Gus signaled for Ty to come over.

Ty hesitated, then set his buckets down and crossed over to the bar. He stopped several feet in front of the two men and looked hard at their feet.

"Hey, kid," Lucy said in a manner so friendly that Ty looked up to see if it had come from someone else. Lucy pointed the crowbar at him. "I got a deal for you."

CHAPTER ELEVEN

"GUS TELLS ME YOUR brother wants to spend a little quality time with you," Lucy said. "Take you to the NFL draft?"

Ty glanced at Uncle Gus and nodded.

"So I think that'd be a good idea," Lucy said. "Truth is, I'm a big fan of Tiger's. I'd like to meet him, make him feel welcome to come here any time. I heard them talking on WFAN that he might be the first pick of the Jets. Imagine that? He'd be pretty close by, right? So I'm thinking, hey, why couldn't he be kind of a regular here?"

Lucy slapped Uncle Gus's back and then gripped his neck while he poked his big belly with the curved end of the crowbar. "So I got your uncle here to let you have your little ESPN outing. How's that for the beginning of a friendship between you and me? Pretty nice guy, huh?"

The red spot on Lucy's face glared at Ty, practically demanding to be looked at. Ty forced himself to stare into Lucy's dark, empty eyes.

"Yes," he said in a small squeak.

"That's right," Lucy said. "Just like your fairy godmother or something, sending you to the ball."

Lucy waved the crowbar like a wand. Uncle Gus forced a smile that lasted until Lucy let go of his neck.

Without thinking, Ty said, "I'd have a lot more to talk about with my brother if Uncle Gus thought it was okay for me to play in the spring passing scrimmage tomorrow."

"What's the spring passing scrimmage?" Lucy asked.

"They have spring football at Halpern Middle," Ty said, avoiding his uncle's eyes. "I'm pretty fast."

Lucy held up his empty hand and jabbed a loose fist at Ty. Ty ducked instinctively and circled right back up. Lucy grinned.

"Not bad," he said, patting Ty's shoulder before he turned his attention to Uncle Gus. "Why can't he play tomorrow? I like the idea."

Uncle Gus sputtered for a moment before he said, "No reason at all. I didn't know he wanted to. Sure."

Lucy winked at Ty. "All right. Go on. I'll see you Monday."

On their way out, Mike looked up from the grill, where two hamburger patties sizzled.

"Gus, how about a fresh donut?" Mike asked.

"Running late," Uncle Gus said, waving him off. "Thanks, Mike. Next time."

Ty shrugged at the big cook and hurried outside.

"Cute, kid. Real cute," Uncle Gus said as he started up his truck. "Fairy godmother, my butt."

Uncle Gus didn't talk about the ESPN draft show all night, but when they finally got home around midnight, he told Charlotte to go inside without them. Ty watched Aunt Virginia come out to greet Charlotte with a kiss as she climbed the stack of cinder blocks. Then the two of them disappeared through the front door. Outside the truck, the crickets chirped. The moon shone down, glimmering off the hood until a cloud swept across it, leaving them alone in the green glow of the dashboard clock.

"You ever see *The Godfather*?" Uncle Gus asked. A small piece of American cheese clung to one of the bristles above his lip.

Ty shook his head. "That's rated R."

"Probably not *The Sopranos* either, huh?" Uncle Gus said.

"I know what it's about," Ty said. "Before I moved down here, my friend Noah told me about that show 'cause he said that's where I was going. North Jersey, right?"

"North Jersey, yeah," Uncle Gus said.

"The mafia."

"Killers, thieves, thugs, drug runners."

Ty kept quiet.

"We don't want those kind of people mad at us, right?" Uncle Gus said.

"No."

"Or mad at your brother," Uncle Gus said. "So all the stuff about Tiger meeting Lucy and maybe hanging out there once in a while? That's secret stuff, get it? You don't talk about it, not with anyone. Especially not Tiger."

"Okay," Ty said.

"You just let it happen. You say something about Lucy being connected to the mafia and Tiger says something, like to a reporter or a cop?" Uncle Gus frowned and shook his head. "You don't know what kind of bad things could happen. But I can count on you, right?"

"Yes."

Uncle Gus put a hand on Ty's leg and Ty pulled away instinctively.

"Okay, then," Uncle Gus said. "Go to bed."

"I can play tomorrow?" Ty asked, opening the truck door and dropping to the ground.

Uncle Gus gripped the steering wheel, narrowed his close-set milky eyes at Ty, and asked, "What makes you think you can just show up and play? You went to one practice. You think you can just show up?"

"Maybe," Ty said. "Coach V likes me."

"Yeah, well, I doubt that's gonna matter," Uncle Gus said, offering up a mean smile. "But I guess we'll see, won't we?"

CHAPTER TWELVE

SATURDAY MORNING DAWNED GRAY and damp, but Ty bounced out of bed and eagerly split half a cord of wood before Aunt Virginia called him inside to eat what was left of the stiffened oatmeal in her saucepan. Afterward, Ty whistled a tune while he helped Uncle Gus change the oil in the pickup truck, even though he had to lie down in the mud and slide in under the truck to catch the dirty oil in an empty milk carton. After a late lunch of Uncle Gus's half-eaten leftover ham sandwich, Ty ran out to use the Porta Potti, then retreated to the laundry room, where he washed his hands and laced his shoes up tight.

When he returned to the kitchen, he was disturbed to see Uncle Gus out in the living room, sitting in his chair, popping open a beer can, and growling at the baseball game.

"Uncle Gus," he said timidly. "The game's at two."

Uncle Gus looked at his watch and scratched the thatch of gray and white hair on his head. "Well, it's in the top of the last inning. You can be a little late."

He sipped at his beer and Ty retreated, walking slowly backward into the kitchen. Aunt Virginia looked up from the sink while her hands continued to scrub a pot.

"What's that look for?" she said. "You crying?"

"No," Ty said with an angry sniff, pushing up his glasses.

"Well, what's wrong?" she asked. "He's letting you go with your brother, I heard."

"I was supposed to play in the spring scrimmage," he said quietly so his uncle couldn't hear him.

"What scrimmage?"

"Football. There's a spring passing scrimmage. Uncle Gus said I could go."

"*Uncle Gus said I could go,*" she said in a whiney imitation of him. "I thought girls were supposed to be the difficult ones. Your cousin never gives us this kind of grief. Where do you think she is right now? In her room reading, that's where. Not making any trouble. Oh, stop looking like that, will you?"

Aunt Virginia removed her hands from the soapy water and picked up a towel, wiping them clean as she walked through the doorway to the living room.

"Gus?" she said. "Gus! Take this boy to his game, would you?"

"I'm watching *baseball*. I said, when I'm done."

"They ain't gonna hold the game for this skinny chicken. Take him now before I bust an artery looking at him. I can't stand those puppy eyes."

Uncle Gus glanced at the window and said, "It's raining."

"They *play* football in the rain."

Aunt Virginia marched right into the middle of the room, snapped off the TV, and turned to face Uncle Gus with her hands on her wide hips. Her face was as red as her hands, and a wisp of her frizzy hair had escaped from behind one ear to hang at an angle across one of the big lenses of her owl glasses. Uncle Gus grumbled, but up he got and disappeared into the bedroom. Ty heard the rattle of his key chain, and he dashed into the living room to give Aunt Virginia a quick hug before bursting through the front door and scurrying to the truck.

Uncle Gus didn't talk, but he brought his beer can with him, sipping at it from time to time and belching with a wide mouth in Ty's direction. When they pulled up to the back of the school, the football team had already spread out on the field to stretch. Small clusters of parents in lawn chairs had set themselves up along the sideline. Some carried umbrellas. Others sat in the small wooden bleachers under bright-colored rain ponchos. Coach V stood in the center of it all wearing a Rutgers cap and blowing on his whistle.

Ty hopped out into the drizzle as soon as Uncle Gus pulled over to the curb.

"Nobody's wearing any pads," Uncle Gus said.

"It's two-hand touch," Ty said. "Just a scrimmage. Passing only."

Uncle Gus grumbled something about dancing around like a bunch of fairies, then said, "I'll be at the Iron Horse Pub. You can walk over there when you're done. It's in the center of town, next to the hotel."

Ty grinned at him. "Thanks, Uncle Gus."

He slammed the door and sprinted across the grass, dropping down into a hurdler's stretch in the back row, soaking his pants through instantly in the wet grass. Ty followed along with the others. The kids around him stared, but Coach V headed toward Ty and everyone looked away.

Ty stood with the team and reached down for his toes, counting to ten. At seven, he saw Coach V's shoes stop on the grass in front of him.

"Ty," the coach said, "what are you doing?"

Ty looked up and blinked at the tiny drops that spattered his glasses. "Stretching."

"I know that."

"For the passing scrimmage."

Coach V looked off into the gray sky, nodding his

head. "You weren't here all week. You said you couldn't play. Now you show up for the scrimmage?"

"I got permission," Ty said, straightening and talking fast. "I worked hard all week. My brother's coming in tonight for the draft. He's taking me into the city with him. I said it would give us something to talk about and my uncle—well, actually, Lucy. My uncle works for him. He's a man. Lucy. He said it was a good idea and so . . . here I am."

"Here you are," Coach V said, raising his eyebrows above his mirrored glasses. "Okay. You don't know the plays."

"You could just tell me, right?" Ty said. "Or I could just run past the defense every time and go for a touchdown."

"Just run past, huh?"

"I'm fast, right?"

Coach V puckered his mouth. "Well, let's see how it goes. Finish stretching."

Ty paced the sideline behind Coach V, wiping his glasses from time to time on the inside of his shirt. The team had been split into two groups, blue and gold, with one of Coach V's assistants calling plays for the blue team from the opposite side of the field. Players wore pinnies that matched the color of their teams. Calvin West played right cornerback for the blue defense, and Ty couldn't help but watch him.

Every play, Calvin would walk right up to the receiver on his side of the field and knock him around as soon as the ball was snapped, jamming the receiver in the chest with both hands, disrupting any chance of getting out into the pass pattern on time. As a result, even though they had Michael Poyer as their quarterback, Ty's gold team was behind 41–35 when the whistle blew, signaling the end of the third quarter. They needed a touchdown. Ty's shirt and pants clung to his body, soaked by the light rain.

When the gold team got the ball back, Ty couldn't keep himself from tapping Coach V on the back. The coach spun around, and Ty realized that he still wore his sunglasses, even in the rain.

"What?" the coach said with a growl. "Oh, Lewis. Yeah, go in. Play the Z."

"Should I just run past him?" Ty asked, holding his glasses out to the coach.

"If you can," the coach said. "What am I supposed to do with those?"

"Can you put them in your pocket?" Ty asked, handing over the glasses.

Coach V took them, then turned his attention to Michael Poyer, who was already out on the field. Coach V used a series of hand signals to give Poyer the play and Ty ran for the huddle.

The field had been torn up pretty good by the other players' cleats, and Ty's own sneakers squelched in the mud. He stepped tentatively into the small huddle—six instead of the usual eleven because they played the passing scrimmage without any linemen. He placed his hands on his knees like the rest of his teammates.

"Right Pro Right, 719, boot pass at eight on two," Poyer said.

"Ready," they all said together, "break!"

Ty hustled to the line and stared up at Calvin. Calvin grinned wide when he recognized Ty, and he flexed his fingers up in the air for Ty to see. Ty tucked in his lower lip and clamped down. He breathed hard through his nose, planning the quick move—faking one way, then darting back the other—that he would use to leave Calvin in his tracks.

Poyer snapped the ball.

Ty ducked, then darted. Calvin struck him dead center in his chest with both hands.

CHAPTER THIRTEEN

TY'S SNEAKERS SLIPPED OUT from under him and down he went, flat on his back. Calvin grabbed his own mouth and howled, doubling over and pointing at Ty as Michael Poyer threw the ball wildly up into the air for an interception.

Calvin ran and grabbed a teammate, pointing at Ty and continuing to howl. Ty hopped up, slipped again, and tumbled back down into the mud. His hands and face were slick and cool with it. This time, he got up slower and jogged to the sideline as the gold defense streamed out onto the field. He looked at Coach V, who simply twisted his mouth up and shook his head.

"That's okay, buddy," the coach said. "Don't worry. Football's not for everyone."

Ty stumbled, suddenly dizzy enough so that he felt

behind him for the wooden plank of the bench and sat down.

One Saturday when Ty was just ten, he and his parents watched Thane drop a pass in the end zone that lost the game for Syracuse. In a sea of fifty thousand people dressed in orange and blue, Ty and his parents were the only ones who didn't boo. Tears blurred Ty's image of the faces in the crowd as his parents dragged him out through the waves of growling fans who spilled from the stadium. The next day, Sunday, while his parents visited a friend in the hospital, Thane showed up at the house unexpectedly with a big bag of laundry.

"Thought I'd clean some clothes," Thane said. "You okay?"

"I'm okay," Ty said. He followed his brother downstairs into the basement, where their mom kept the washing machine.

"You don't look okay," Thane said, glancing back as he stuffed some clothes into the machine.

"I just feel bad. That's all."

"About the game?" Thane asked, turning to his wash.

"The same people who cheer, now they're booing at you?" Ty said. "That's not right."

Thane surprised him with a smile. "That's the game."

Thane let the top of the machine fall closed with a

bang. He turned around and knelt down in front of Ty, putting his hands on his shoulders, the smell of laundry soap heavy in the air.

"Yesterday? That stinks, but football is about getting up," Thane said, his hazel eyes glinting even in the dim light. "Anyone could do it if you caught touchdown passes every time and the crowd cheered for you in the end zone. That's not what makes you a football player.

"What makes you a football player is getting up after you get knocked down, or going out to catch another pass after you just dropped one. The harder the hit, or the worse the drop, the more important it is to keep going. That's the game. That's what a real football player does. If you can't do that, then you shouldn't play."

Ty sprang up off the bench. He poked Coach V in the ribs until he looked down.

"Put me back in, Coach," he said. "I can do it."

Coach V hesitated.

"Everyone gets knocked down," Ty said. "It's about getting up."

A smile crept into the corners of the coach's lips.

"Okay," he said, "go."

Ty slipped out of his shoes and stripped off his socks.

"What are you—" Coach V started to say.

Before he could finish, Ty sprinted out into the huddle and tapped the Z receiver on the back, telling the boy that Coach V had sent him in.

Then he looked at Poyer and said, "Run the nine."

The quarterback looked at Ty's bare feet, then to the sideline.

"Run it!" Ty said. "I'll be open."

"Let's go!" Coach V shouted with his hands cupped around his mouth.

Poyer called the play and Ty sprinted to the line, setting his feet and looking back in at the quarterback. From the corner of his eye, he saw Calvin saunter up with his hands on his hips.

"Looking to get knocked on your butt again?" Calvin asked.

Ty scowled and set his mouth.

"Oooh, I'm scared," Calvin said. "You look so mean. You shoeless beggar."

Ty clenched his hands, then flexed his fingers as Poyer started his cadence. At the snap, Ty darted inside, turning his shoulders to narrow the target Calvin could punch at. A hand grazed Ty's back and he slipped by, surging up the field. Two steps later, he felt a jolt in his neck and he was nearly yanked off his feet.

Calvin had grabbed hold of his gold pinnie—illegal, but effective.

Ty leaned forward and kept digging in his feet,

despite the sharp pain in his throat.

A loud rip set him free. Calvin looked at the torn pinnie a moment too long. Ty sprang forward and sprinted toward the end zone. An instant later, the ball was in the air, a long, high arc, too far for Ty to reach.

Then, he found something deep, another gear, another surge of energy, of speed.

Ty ran as fast as he could run. His lungs burned and his joints seemed to melt. He looked back.

The ball came down fast.

CHAPTER FOURTEEN

TY STRETCHED EVERY FIBER. He felt the sharp ache of straining ligaments in his shoulders. His fingers touched the ball, saving it from the ground the way a desperate flipper keeps a pinball in play. His eyes locked on it like a laser-sighted weapons system, following the arc of the ball as it tilted wildly, redirecting his hands so they could keep it from hitting the ground.

His left hand connected, fingers groping, but the ball had a mind of its own and sprang into the air once again. His right hand reined it in. The left caught up. He had it between his hands, and his feet kept moving, catching him from tumbling to the wet grass. One, two, three long, off-balance strides and he was back up, running full speed into the end zone.

Ty slowed and raised the ball in one hand, turning, erect, chin up, and grinning at his teammates fifty yards away, moving toward him in a ragtag heap, cheering wildly, spinning and dancing and bouncing. Even without his glasses, Ty could see the glow of Coach V's smile from the sideline.

A cigarette hung from Uncle Gus's lower lip, suspended there by some unknown force, tipping at an angle that promised to tickle his chin with its burning ember. His eyes were half closed. Two empty pint glasses stood next to a third, where only a bit of foamy beer remained. His head jerked up and his upper lip pinned down the cigarette to its lower sister, hiding the filter in his weedy mustache.

"What?" he said, squinting through the tendril of smoke.

"I'm finished," Ty said. "I caught a touchdown pass. I won the game."

"*I won the game,*" Uncle Gus said, mimicking him with a high-pitched whine.

"Thank you, Uncle Gus."

"*Thank you Uncle Gus,*" he said, brushing pretzel crumbs off his chest, then stubbing out his cigarette as he stood to go. "*I'm sorry I wasted your Saturday afternoon.*"

"I'm sorry if I did," Ty said, unable to extinguish his happiness completely.

"They let you play, huh?" Uncle Gus said, pulling a limp five-dollar bill from his wallet and flopping it down on the bar. Then he froze and pointed at Ty's muddy, bare feet.

"I kept slipping," Ty said, "so I took off my sneakers."

"Humph," Uncle Gus said, shaking his head and heading toward the door.

As they drove, Ty replayed the touchdown catch over and over in his mind. The fresh cigarette smoke barely registered with him, even though his uncle kept the windows up because of the rain. Ty recalled Coach V's thick, callused hand pumping his own while he patted him on the back with the other. He remembered the faces of the parents, peering out at him from under umbrellas and hooded raincoats, pointing and whispering. He even heard someone call him Tiger Lewis's brother, and the memory of that sent a chill down his spine.

"So you just keep smiling like that when you see your brother tonight," his uncle said from out of nowhere.

"I'll be happy to see him," Ty said.

"I got a business idea for him," Uncle Gus said. "It'd be good for the family. That's you, too, right?"

"Yes," Ty said, shifting in his seat. "But Thane's a biology major."

"That means he can't go into business?" Uncle Gus said angrily. "You don't have to have a college degree to be in business. Lucy's a millionaire and he dropped out in the tenth grade. Don't talk to me about biology."

"Okay," Ty said, and they rode in silence the rest of the way home, splashing through the muddy puddles along the track that led through the weeds and coming to rest beside the blue tarp extending from one side of the low, crooked house.

"Split a cord of that wood, then get cleaned up before your brother gets here," Uncle Gus said, slipping out into the rain without looking back.

Ty sighed and climbed down from the truck. As he swung the ax, he pretended it was part of a training regimen Coach V had put him on to get ready for the season, counting out his strokes as he hacked away.

Under the blue tarp, Aunt Virginia filled half an old oil drum with water from a garden hose. The drum, split down the middle and tipped on its side, left a fine silt of rust floating on the water's surface that sparkled on Ty's skin long after a bath. To avoid total humiliation, Ty kept his underwear on, even though Aunt Virginia always pursed her lips and declared she'd seen it all anyway. When he got out of the bath, Ty hurried back inside, shivering, and dried off on the washroom floor. Atop the washing machine, Aunt Virginia had laid out a set of clothes normally reserved for church.

From the kitchen came the warm, delicious smell of cooking caramel.

Ty winced as he buttoned up the white shirt with its stiff collar and wedged his feet into a pair of old brown shoes that came from the Salvation Army. He knew better than to argue, and a part of him thought it was only right to dress this way for something as important as Thane's being drafted into the NFL. Ty parted his hair on the side and combed it straight the way he knew his aunt liked it.

He followed the smell of hot caramel into the tiny kitchen, where his aunt shooed him away from the steaming pot on the stove. He then wandered into the living room, where Uncle Gus had taken up his usual spot in the musty old reclining chair directly in front of the TV. Uncle Gus took a swig of beer from his can, belched, and looked up at Ty with glassy eyes.

"Sit down," he said, waving his can at the couch. "I got an idea."

Ty sat.

"We can call it Tiger's, after him," Uncle Gus said, slurring his words a bit.

"What, Uncle Gus?"

"Tiger's, or Tiger's Place, or Tiger's Lair. I like that, but I'll even let him decide."

"A place?"

"A bar," Uncle Gus said. "I told you, Lucy, he's a millionaire. A bar with a little gambling action on the side. That's how you do it. You think I want to clean crappers for the rest of my life? Do you?"

Ty shook his head.

"I read it in the news," Uncle Gus said, grabbing a handful of the morning paper from the floor beside his chair and rattling it in the air. "They say he might go to the Jets! The third pick! His signing bonus, six, seven, eight million dollars!"

Ty swallowed and pushed himself back into the couch.

"We could get a class place up and going for a couple hundred thousand," Uncle Gus said. "Maybe three hundred thousand. What's that to him? Nothing. Not now."

Ty felt the excitement of seeing his brother drain out of him, replaced by a tightness that made him start to sweat.

"What's that look?" Uncle Gus said, glowering, the vein in his forehead beginning to show. "You don't want to help?"

Ty didn't know what to say. His head went up and down and back and forth, jiggling like a baby's toy. The rumble of a big engine from out front saved him. Charlotte shot into the room, flinging aside the curtains so she could see out.

"He's here," she said. "Look at that limo."

Uncle Gus gave Ty a final scowl as he struggled up out of his chair and stumbled to the front window. Ty followed, peeking out. Even under the cloudy sky, the stretch Hum-V limousine gleamed like a jewel with its sparkling chrome grill, hood ornament, and rims. The long black side reflected a perfect image of the house that looked like a trailer and the trees beyond. The back door popped open, and Thane, or Tiger, as Uncle Gus said in a whisper, hopped out and strode up the broken slate path toward the front door.

CHAPTER FIFTEEN

THANE STOOD SIX FEET, two inches tall with broad shoulders and a long torso that dropped to a narrow waist. He wore a new, dark blue Nike sweat suit with white turf shoes from Syracuse University that had orange stripes. His hair, brown with a hint of red, was swept back off his face and fell in waves all the way past his collar. His nose was narrow, long, and straight above a delicate mouth that broke out into an easy smile when he saw Ty poking out from behind Uncle Gus in the doorway.

Ty felt the warmth from Thane's hazel eyes. Their look reminded him of his parents, and that immediately choked him up so that he couldn't speak, even when Thane asked him how he was doing.

"He's great," Uncle Gus said, grinning wider than

Ty had ever seen. "Look at *that* ride. Tiger Lewis has arrived."

Thane blushed and looked at Ty, mussing his hair.

"ESPN sent it," Thane said. "You ready, pal?"

Ty nodded.

"Oh, you have to come in," Uncle Gus said, "for a minute anyway. Your aunt made caramel apples, just for you. If the Jets pick you first, you'll be a big hero around here. You can't not come in. Maybe we could take a family picture. Then one for Charlotte that she can take to school. Ty, too. You'd like that, wouldn't you, Ty?"

Uncle Gus had his hand on Ty's shoulder and it tightened as he spoke.

Ty nodded again, Thane shrugged, and they went inside.

The living room seemed even smaller with Thane standing there, his head nearly touching the brown water stain on the ceiling. Uncle Gus offered Thane a beer. Thane smiled, shaking his head and holding up a hand to say no thanks. Aunt Virginia came out with her apron on, carrying a tray with a dozen caramel apples lined up in four rows of three.

"Sit, sit," Uncle Gus said, offering Thane his chair.

Thane sat next to Ty on the couch and took an apple. Ty reached for one, saw his aunt grimace, and pulled back his hand. Thane stopped just as he was about to bite into his apple and looked at their aunt, who flashed a big smile.

"Go ahead, Ty," she said. "Take one. He loves candy, doesn't he?"

Ty wanted to say he hadn't had a piece of candy in six months but figured it would be best to keep quiet. Charlotte and Uncle Gus grabbed apples, too. Aunt Virginia set the tray down on the coffee table and stepped back. That seemed to be the signal to begin, because they all bit into their apples, snapping away hunks of the crisp fruit coated in sticky caramel. Ty closed his eyes and let the warm sweetness melt in his mouth and drizzle down the back of his throat.

After his second bite, Thane set his apple back down on the tray, explaining that his training called for him to watch every single thing that went into his body.

When Thane saw Ty frowning at his apple, he said, "Don't you worry. You don't have to start doing the diet thing until you're in college."

"I'm gonna play in college, too, you know," Ty said, blurting out the words so fast he choked on a hunk of apple.

"Easy," Thane said, patting him on the back.

They talked for a few minutes about the draft while Ty gobbled the caramel apple down to the core before setting the wooden stick back down on the tray. Thane told them about the combines, a place where the top three hundred college players went to be measured, weighed, examined, and tested by all thirty-one NFL teams' doctors, training staffs, and coaches.

"They treat you like hamburger," Thane said.

"But now you get paid," Uncle Gus said with a wink before taking the last bite of his apple and a swig from his beer can. "And when you do, I've got a little business proposition for you."

Thane stiffened and said, "I don't want to spend any money until I've got it, Uncle Gus, and right now I've got two hundred and seventy-three dollars in my bank account. That's it. So, unless you're thinking about a lemonade stand or a paper route, let's just put it on hold."

Uncle Gus jerked back with a look of shock on his face. He touched his fingers to his big gut and said, "I'd never try to push you into anything. Don't get me wrong, Tiger. When you're ready, that's all. It's something you're going to want to do with someone, I'm sure. And so, when you do it, I'm just hoping we can do it together. Better with family than someone you can't trust. That's a good idea, right?"

"Sure," Thane said, slapping his knees and standing up. "Well, let's do those pictures. We've got to get into the city. We're meeting my agent for dinner and I don't want to be late."

They took a bunch of pictures in the living room, and Thane smiled patiently like a pro before leading Ty out to the limo. Ty glanced back at his new family, waving to him from the cinder-block stoop like they never had before. Ty gave them a quick wave, then ducked into the back of the limo, sitting on the bench seat along the side and marveling at the TV, the rows of tiny golden lights along the ceiling, and the twinkling glasses lined up on the bar. In the front, a mirror surrounding the small opening into the front seat reflected the image back at them and made the string of lights on the ceiling appear to go on forever.

Thane yelled good-bye, then climbed in and closed the door.

"Whew," Thane said. "You okay?"

Ty nodded.

"To dinner, Mr. Lewis?" the driver asked, his voice sounding small from all the way up front.

"Sounds good, Randy," Thane said. "Randy, my brother Ty. Ty, Randy."

The driver looked back through the small opening and waved, then put the big machine into gear, easing out of the front yard and down the rutted track.

"Come on over here," Thane said, patting the seat beside him.

Ty shifted into the back. Thane put an arm around him and hugged him close, kissing him on top of his head the way their father used to do to both of them.

Ty heard his brother sniff, and when Thane took a deep breath it was ragged and he realized that Thane was crying.

"It'd make them happy to see you and me like this, wouldn't it?" Thane asked. "A big limousine? Tomorrow, a big day?"

Ty looked up at his brother's face and the tears streaming down his cheeks. He felt his own tears well up in his eyes, and even though Thane cried first, he held them back as long as he could before burying his nose into Thane's sweat suit and letting go.

He wrapped his arms around Thane's iron stomach and hung on. Thane kept crying, and he held Ty so tight it almost hurt.

After a time, Thane took a series of deep, slow breaths and the two of them separated. He kept his arm around Ty, though, as he wiped his eyes on his sleeve. Ty did the same thing on his stiff dress shirt.

"You okay?" Thane asked after a minute.

Ty nodded, looking out the long window at the Manhattan skyline as they approached the Lincoln Tunnel.

"Okay," Thane said. "'Cause I got a surprise for you."

CHAPTER SIXTEEN

THANE TOOK A PIECE of paper from the pocket of his sweat jacket and unfolded it, reading the address in a voice that Randy, the driver, could hear. The car came up out of the tunnel and headed north, through the mountain range of skyscrapers. Up ahead, Ty saw trees.

"What's that?" he asked.

"Central Park," Thane said. "It's huge. It's like they took a hunk of Tully and dropped it down right in the middle of all this concrete. There's trees, streams, ponds, hills, rocks, birds, you name it."

"Raccoons?"

"Plenty."

"Wow," Ty said, pressing his nose to the window as they turned right and the trees disappeared. "Where are we going now?"

"First the surprise," Thane said. "Then the restaurant, then the Palace."

"Palace?"

"It's a hotel."

"Is it like a palace?" Ty asked, looking at his brother's smiling face.

"For us it is," Thane said.

The house they both grew up in was a small two-story, three-bedroom colonial off a rural highway. Their home wasn't a dump like Uncle Gus and Aunt Virginia's, but it wasn't any palace, either. Out back, though, you could see for miles across the Tully Valley, and Ty's dad always said it was a million-dollar view.

The Hum-V limo pulled over on Fifth Avenue. Thane got out and waited for Ty on the sidewalk, looking up. The building looked like the big square tower of a castle, red brick with flags flying on the ramparts above. The front was filled almost entirely by a huge glass arched window. Above the entryway, big silver metal letters declared the place to be Niketown. Thane grabbed Ty by the arm and led him inside.

Ty stared in wonder at all the stuff and all the enormous pictures of famous athletes covering the walls and at the signs and banners that were everywhere. A pretty woman with a ponytail saw them looking and asked if she could help.

"I want to get my man here a nice sweat suit,"

Thane said. "Something with style."

"Over here," she said, walking through the displays and stopping at a rack of black sweat suits. "It's called the Control Sweat Suit, my favorite."

"You like that?" Thane asked.

Ty's mouth hung open. He just nodded.

"Let's see, you look like a youth, medium. You want to try it on?"

"He's gonna wear it out of here," Thane said. "And can you get a pair of the new Pro Shock shoes? Size seven, right, Ty?"

The woman nodded, pointed out the dressing rooms, and disappeared.

"Thane," Ty said, looking at the price tag. "You said you only had two hundred seventy-three dollars. This and the shoes is all the money you have."

Thane grinned, and his hazel eyes twinkled like tiny Christmas-tree lights.

"Morty, my agent?" Thane said. "He gave me a credit card."

"You said you don't spend anything you don't have."

"Buddy, in about twenty hours, I'm gonna have more money than either of us ever dreamed of. Don't worry about it. I gotta get you out of that church gear. It's strangling you."

Ty tugged at the collar of his white shirt. He sighed and shrugged and said, "Thane, if you are going to get me shoes, can I get football cleats instead, as long as they're not more than the Pro Shock shoes?"

"Football cleats? You can't wear them around."

"I need them more than the Pro Shock shoes, though," Ty said, remembering the feel of the cold mud on his bare feet. "To play."

Thane knelt down in front of him and rested his forearms on Ty's shoulders. "I'm gonna get you both. You don't have to worry about that."

Ty shook his head and said, "I don't want to be a mooch."

"You're my brother," Thane said, standing up. "And for your information, a mooch is someone who asks. Uncle Gus, that's a mooch. You're not like that. Now go put this on. I'll have her get you some cleats when she gets back."

Thane looked at his watch. "We got dinner in twenty minutes, so stop standing there."

Ty shut the dressing room door and wiggled out of his church clothes, slipping into the silky sweat suit just as Thane handed the box of Pro Shock shoes in under the door. When he came out, Thane and the saleswoman started clapping.

"Now you're ready," Thane said.

Thane paid with the credit card, and the woman put Ty's church clothes into the Nike bag along with the cleats. The limo took them to a fancy restaurant called Fresco by Scotto. A nice older woman greeted them and nodded when Thane mentioned Morty

Wolkoff. She led them into the crowded dining room, where waiters in black ties slipped between tables covered by white linen, fresh flowers, flickering candles, and glimmering silverware.

Thane's agent sat at a table along the wall, on the cushioned bench, talking on his cell phone. His hair was thin and graying, his face round and flushed, with a sharp nose, and he, too, wore a silky sweat suit. His gold watch gleamed like his white smile, and Ty liked him before he even spoke.

Morty snapped the phone shut and his words came out in rapid fire.

"Now, it might not be the Jets," he said, looking at Thane with his eyebrows knit.

"What?" Thane said, amazement on his face. "I thought it was practically a done deal? What'd you find out?"

"You're not going to like it," Morty said.

CHAPTER SEVENTEEN

MORTY SAID, "THEY HAD Jack MacDougal, the wide receiver from Tennessee, in for a workout yesterday afternoon. He ran a 4.21 forty."

Thane's mouth tightened into a flat line.

"What's that?" Ty asked, unable to keep the words in his mouth.

"The forty-yard dash is how teams measure your speed," Morty said. "Tiger's fast, he ran a 4.26, it's amazing. This other receiver, he doesn't have as many catches as Tiger. His hands aren't as good and he's not as tough, but he's two inches taller, and with that kind of speed, the Jets might use their pick on him."

Thane and Ty sat down across from Morty. Ty saw the cloud of concern pass over his brother's face before it returned to normal.

"It's, like, .05 seconds," Ty said.

"Which is a lot," Thane said, "believe it or not."

"I don't know," Morty said, "maybe it's a trick to keep the Cardinals from using the second pick to get you."

"The Cardinals don't need a receiver," Thane said.

"Maybe they've got a trade cooking," Morty said. "You never know with them."

"If he doesn't get picked third, will he get picked fourth?" Ty asked.

"It doesn't work that way," Morty said. "The Jets need a receiver. The next team who'd use their first-round pick for a receiver might not be until Atlanta, although I could see San Diego taking you, too, with the tenth pick."

"He'll still be a first-round pick, though, right?" Ty asked.

Morty tilted his head and nodded. "Yeah, but the Falcons pick twenty-seventh. The difference between third and twenty-seventh is about twenty million dollars over the first four years of the contract."

Ty's mouth hung open and he looked up at his brother. "What about the Giants? Could they pick you? Then you'd still be right here."

"I doubt the Giants," Morty said. "The Patriots, maybe, but I doubt the Giants."

Thane shrugged and said, "Nothing we can do, right? Let's eat."

"Maybe I shouldn't have told you," Morty said, looking sadly at his cell phone.

"No," Thane said, cracking open a menu and sounding genuinely unconcerned. "That's okay. It's better to be ready."

"You will be a first-round pick," Morty said. "Tomorrow at this time, you'll be a millionaire. That's the good news. It's just a matter of how many millions you have. Not a bad problem when you look at it like that, right?"

"Right," Thane said.

They were all quiet for a few minutes, then Morty set his menu down and started asking Ty questions about school and if he, too, was a football player. Ty said he was.

"I'll sign you up now, then, right?" Morty said, grinning big.

After they ordered, Thane excused himself to the restroom.

Morty watched Thane go, then he leaned toward Ty and his eyes lost some of their merry sparkle.

"Can I talk to you?" he asked.

"Sure," Ty said, picking a long, thin breadstick out of its silver basket and crunching on it.

"You and Tiger, you get along good, huh?" Morty said.

"He's my brother," Ty said. "I call him Thane."

"And you wouldn't want anything bad to happen to him, right?" Morty said.

Ty set the breadstick down. "No. Why?"

"I know you're young—"

"I'm twelve."

"Yeah. Well, wherever he gets drafted, Tiger's going to have a lot of money and I don't want to see him lose it all the way most guys do. You know what I mean?"

Ty shook his head and shrugged. "What are you talking about?"

Morty sat back and took a fat roll of money out of his pocket. He peeled a bill off the outside, a hundred-dollar bill. He held it up and snapped it tight.

"This," he said. "It changes everything. Guys like Tiger, they want to help everyone. They got a little brother who needs a new sweat suit, a pair of sneakers? Fine. But what happens is that it never ends. The whole family lines up with these NFL players. Mom wants a new house. Wouldn't Dad look great driving a Cadillac? Uncle Zemo's ready to open a sports bar. Aunt Jenny needs a hair transplant."

"You know about the bar?"

"What bar?" Morty said, raising his eyebrows.

"Uncle Gus, he said something to Thane about it."

"See?" Morty said, snapping the bill again. "It never stops. The bars and restaurants, they always go belly-up. The businesses fail. The money gets spent as fast as it comes in, then taxes take a hit, a guy gets hurt, and he's out of the game with a mortgage he can't afford, no line of work, and what money he has

left is gone in a year or two. Bang, he's a poor slob sell-
ing his Super Bowl ring to pay for a vacation to the
Bahamas. That's if he was lucky enough to go to the
Super Bowl."

Ty bit into his lower lip.

"A lot of agents, they like it that way," Morty said.
"Let the guy spend it all. The agent's got his hand out,
too, getting him into investment deals that he gets a
cut of. I'm not like that. I don't want any money I don't
earn."

Morty's eyes softened.

"I know you don't want that either. I see you care
about your brother, right?" Morty said, wrapping the
bill back onto the outside of the wad and replacing it
in his pocket. "That's why I'm saying something. Don't
let it happen. I can tell by the way he looks at you that
if you asked, there's nothing he wouldn't give you, but
don't. You gotta live your life. You got school. You got
food, clothes, a roof over your head, right? That's all
anyone needs. You gotta make your own way after
that. Trust me.

"The other way? It never works."

Thane appeared suddenly, sitting down and asking, "What are you guys talking so serious about?"

CHAPTER EIGHTEEN

"YOU," MORTY SAID TO Thane. "Your brother is worried about you. What's this thing about your uncle and a bar? I told you about all that, right?"

Thane waved his hand in the air and sipped at a glass of sparkling water. "He's not so bad. Don't worry. I'm not getting into anything like that."

"'Cause I told you, right?" Morty said.

"You know," Thane said, "our dad worked hard his whole life. He was an electrician, worked for himself. Had a pretty nice retirement plan he saved up. Had the house almost all paid off. Then he lost everything in the stock market, bought a bunch of AOL. I'll be putting my money in the bank, thank you."

"Good," Morty said. "Now we don't have to worry."

The food came and Ty remembered how much he

liked to eat. He had pasta with tomato sauce, then a steak with mushrooms. The flavors filled his mouth, and juice from the meat dribbled down his chin. For dessert, they had homemade ice cream and Italian cannoli, a thin cookie tube filled with a creamy center that tasted so good, Ty had to close his eyes when he bit into it. When they were finished, Ty was so full he could barely walk out the door. They said good-bye to Morty, who waved and disappeared into a cab.

The rain had stopped. High above, shreds of white clouds sailed across the sky like ghosts. Thane asked if he wanted to walk off some of the food and take a stroll up to the park.

"Sure," Ty said.

Thane went to the window of the limo and told Randy that if he could drop off his suitcase and Ty's bag at the hotel, then they would just see him tomorrow. The gray street was like a narrow canyon between the rows of skyscrapers, but the sidewalks were wide and nearly empty of people. Thane rested his hand on Ty's shoulder, and they walked for a couple blocks without saying anything.

Finally, Thane asked, "You like Morty?"

"Yes," Ty said as they turned onto Fifth Avenue, heading for the park. "He's got a lot of money."

"That's 'cause he's a good agent," Thane said. "Honest."

"Seems like that," Ty said, stopping to stare at the

massive gold statue of a winged angel leading a soldier on horseback. The statue marked a corner of Central Park. It shimmered under the city lights, and Ty found his feet moving toward it, wanting to reach out and touch it. But when he got closer, he realized that its granite base was much bigger than it looked and even the angel's feet were out of reach.

"Pretty awesome," Thane said, looking up. "Come on."

They crossed the street between a thin stream of black limousines and yellow taxicabs and stood at the top of a stone stairway that led down into the park. Even though he could see the streetlights glinting up through the trees, there was something eerie about the dark descent and the black pool of water Ty could see beyond the path.

"Is it safe?" Ty asked.

"Sure," Thane said.

But the two of them stood there, looking.

"It's kind of dark," Ty said.

Thane walked down a couple steps and turned around, facing Ty so that they were eye to eye. He put his hand on Ty's shoulder and gave it a squeeze.

"Hey," he said. "I want to talk to you."

"Sure."

"You heard everything Morty said about me getting picked in the first round," Thane said. "It's gonna happen. I'm gonna be kind of rich."

"Sounds that way," Ty said.

"So, if I'm rich, you are, too," Thane said. "I know we don't talk about Mom and Dad. We're the same that way; it's too soon to talk about it. One day we will, but it hurts too much now."

Ty nodded and gripped the metal railing at the top of the steps. He scowled and his throat tightened.

"Sometimes I dream about the things we used to do together," Ty said. "You know, camping and stuff, but I can't see them. I know they're there, and I see you, but I just can't see *them*."

"You will one day," Thane said quietly before he cleared his throat. "And they'd be happy to know I've got you covered. So, anything you need, you just got to let me know. Uncle Gus and Aunt Virginia, they're okay, I guess. But you need something, you gotta tell me, okay?"

Ty swallowed and looked up at his older brother. The invitation twinkled in his eyes, reflecting the light from the golden angel across the street. Ty knew he meant it. All he had to do was tell him about Uncle Gus and the cleaning business and not being allowed to play football and his brother, the tiger, would smash Uncle Gus like a bug, maybe punch him right in the mouth, and he'd take Ty away from all that to live with him in some mansion he'd buy with all the money he was going to make. They'd have a cook to make their meals and a housekeeper to clean their clothes.

All Ty had to do was ask.

CHAPTER NINETEEN

BUT HE COULDN'T.

"I'm doing really good there," Ty said, forcing a smile onto his face.

"You are?" Thane said, his eyebrows drifting up.

"Yeah," Ty said, nodding. "They got a good school. The gym coach says I'm the fastest kid he's got."

"No surprise there," Thane said.

"I have food, clothes, and a roof over my head," Ty said. "That's all you need, right?"

Thane tilted his head, pulling down the corners of his mouth, and nodded at the wisdom of it; then he mussed Ty's hair and walked back up the steps.

"Come on," he said. "Let's go see our palace."

"You don't want to walk in the park?" Ty asked, looking back.

"Nah," Thane said. "It's getting late."

"Maybe there's a Jacuzzi tub?" Ty said.

"Wouldn't surprise me," Thane said.

Uncle Gus's entire house could have fit inside their suite at the Palace. Brass lamps and crystal chandeliers glittered in the midst of rich brown wood paneling. Ty could smell the leather from the furniture. On the long dining room table a pile of gifts from ESPN awaited them. Thane let Ty open them all and told him to keep the watch because he already had one.

"Take all that stuff," Thane said.

"No," Ty said, slipping a new iPod back into its packaging.

"It's free."

"I can't take all of it," Ty said, lifting a hooded sweatshirt out of the pile of clothes. "Maybe something for Uncle Gus and Aunt Virginia and Charlotte. They'd be happy, especially if I told them it was from you."

"Knock yourself out," Thane said, picking up a can of mixed nuts and cracking the seal before he poked through the minibar. He came up with a 7UP for himself and a Coke for Ty before he jumped over the back of the couch and clicked on the TV.

Ty took a swig of soda and put aside a pen-and-pencil set for his aunt, the iPod for Charlotte, and a big leather travel bag for Uncle Gus; then he went into the bedroom.

"Hey!" he shouted out toward the living room. "There *is* a Jacuzzi!"

"Get in it!" Thane shouted from the other room. "This place is for fun!"

Ty ran the water and stripped right down. Big silver buttons gleamed at him from a panel along the marble wall.

"There's tons of buttons!" Ty yelled out over the sound of the water.

"Push 'em all!"

Ty did, and the tub rumbled and spit. Next, he turned to examine all the little things on the white marble vanity between the sinks.

"There's a toothbrush!" Ty shouted through the wall.

"Use it!" came the answer.

Ty grinned at himself and put some paste on the brush and scrubbed his teeth while the bath filled. Then he lowered himself into the bubbling water. He let his head fall back and closed his eyes, soaking up the warmth and letting the jets pound his muscles into butter.

"I could get used to this," he said aloud to himself.

By the time Thane shook him awake, the sun had already cleared the buildings beside the hotel so that thick beams fell in through the curtains.

"Come on, sleepyhead," Thane said. He wore shorts

and a T-shirt so drenched in sweat that it looked as though he'd been dipped in a pool. "I'm going to shower, then we'll get something to eat. The car picks us up at nine-thirty."

"I thought it doesn't start till twelve," Ty said, rubbing the sleep from his eyes.

"TV, man," Thane said, snapping his towel against the covers. "Everything starts before it starts."

"I'm coming," Ty said, swinging his legs out of bed.

Breakfast came right to their room, served by a waiter in a black bow tie who removed fancy silver covers from plates of sausage, scrambled eggs, and toast and who poured fresh-squeezed orange juice from a crystal pitcher. Ty watched his older brother, who dug in as if they were at home or in a diner, and so he did the same, enjoying the food without concern for the fancy surroundings.

The limo took them to the Javits Convention Center VIP entrance, where a woman from the NFL greeted them and led them toward the massive glass building. There were crowds of fans and kids on the other side of the velvet ropes waiting in the sunshine, and Thane stopped to sign dozens of Syracuse Orangemen hats, banners, and collector's helmets. Finally, they were inside and led into a VIP reception area, where players milled about with their agents, families, and people from the NFL.

Morty appeared, looking frazzled. Dark circles

drooped beneath his eyes, and the smile on his face flickered like a loose lightbulb.

"I can't call it. I can't call it," he said, crossing his arms and uncrossing them and holding out his hand to say no to the woman offering him a glass of champagne from a tray. "MacDougal is right over there. Look at that smile. Look at those gold teeth."

Thane buried his hands deep in his pockets looking around at the banners and balloons and tables heavy with food and drinks.

"Man, can you believe all this? This is fun," Thane said with a shiver.

"Fun is when I've got the deal locked down," Morty mumbled. "Come on, let's get to our seats. What took you so long?"

"He signed a bunch of stuff for people," Ty said as Thane put an arm around his shoulder and started to walk toward the exit.

"You gotta stop doing that," Morty said. "People pay for that stuff. After today, I can get you twenty, thirty thousand to show up and sign stuff for a couple hours. You don't want to just do it for free."

"Come on," Thane said, scoffing. "Are you serious?"

Morty looked surprised. "Do I joke about money?"

"I'm not asking people to pay for an autograph," Thane said. "No way. People will be paying me by watching and coming to the games. That's where it comes from."

"We do live in a free market," Morty said. "If people

will pay you for something, you deserve to get it."

"Not me," Thane said. "Not for kids anyway."

Ty nodded in agreement without saying anything.

In front of a stage on one side were several hundred seats for players and their guests. In another section were the desks for all of the NFL teams' representatives. Fans got to sit in the bleachers surrounding the floor. A few thousand were there already, creating a hum of noise that added to the excitement. A couple hundred at least were Jets fans, dressed in green and white and holding signs. Many of them flashed Tiger's name, but there were plenty that said "MacDougal." Morty took out three tickets and gave them to an usher, who led them to the front row. When the Jets fans spotted Thane, some burst out into applause that sent a chill down Ty's back.

Thane sat with his hands in the pockets of his sweat jacket, looking around and smiling as if he were on a hayride back home in Tully. Other players began to file in. When Ty held up one of his hands, he saw the tremble in his fingers and he jammed them under his legs. A twitch tugged at the corner of his eye, and there was nothing he could do but hope it would go away. He couldn't keep his eyes from wandering over the different team logos, reciting the cities to himself, seeing them on a map in his mind. Most of them were so far away from New Jersey that Ty knew he'd never see his brother. His heart thumped and his throat tightened.

Before he knew it, the seats around him were packed with people, and the commissioner stepped up to the podium and began the draft. The Lions picked the quarterback from Texas and the Cardinals took the quarterback from Tennessee, so there was no trade in the works. Ty looked over at Morty, who clutched a program in his fist and clenched his teeth. MacDougal was in the third row, surrounded by a big contingent that Ty presumed was his family. The tall, fast wide receiver sat nodding his head, like he knew what was going to happen next.

Thane still looked relaxed, smiling and enjoying himself as much now as when he was signing people's hats outside. The Jets seemed to take forever. In reality, each team had only fifteen minutes to make their pick in the first round. Ty glued his eyes to the Jets' desk. Two men in suits sat whispering to each other. One of them held a phone clutched to his ear.

"What the heck is taking them so long?" Morty muttered.

Finally, one of the men walked up to the stage and handed a sheet of paper to the commissioner, who stepped up to the podium.

"With the third pick of the draft," he said, looking up and searching the crowd.

MacDougal leaned forward in his seat and began to stand up.

CHAPTER TWENTY

THE COMMISSIONER TOOK A breath and continued. "The New York Jets select Tiger Lewis, wide receiver from Syracuse."

Many of the Jets fans exploded with glee, cheering so loud that Ty heard the sound in waves.

Morty jumped up with them, hugging Ty and Thane together. An enormous smile lit Thane's face and tears sparkled in his eyes. Ty didn't know the extent of his own happiness until he felt the tears running freely down his own cheeks.

Charlotte shed the next set of tears. She sat on the edge of her bed, looking down and holding the iPod in both hands as if it were a small animal or a fragile butterfly. Her long dirty blond hair hung in two straight curtains on either side of her face. Ty stood at the foot of the bed with his hands jammed into the pockets of his jeans.

"Do you like it?" Ty asked. "It's preloaded."

"It's," she said, looking up with a sniff and blinking the tears from her big round eyes, "the nicest thing anyone ever gave me."

Ty looked down and nudged a hole in the thin carpet with the toe of his sneaker.

"It's really from Thane," he said. "It was his stuff."

"I feel like the mouse with the lion in that story," she said, sniffling and wiping at the corner of her eye. "What could I ever do this nice for you, right? I don't have a dime to my name. But I will. Some thorn in your foot or something."

An embarrassed smile flickered onto Charlotte's face before she laughed, stuffed the earpieces into her ears, cranked up some music, and began to bob her head to the beat. Then she reached out, took his hand from its pocket, and gave it a squeeze.

Ty felt his cheeks heat up, but he squeezed back, happy to have a friend.

The summer crept along, worse than any summer in Ty's life.

Thane had one more class to get his college degree, and so he stayed at Syracuse University, training and studying. While everyone agreed that Thane's contract would be in the millions, Morty and the Jets couldn't come to terms, and the agent told Thane that he should expect to have to hold out of training camp.

When Ty heard this over the telephone, he said, "So you might not get the money until August?"

"Maybe even September," Thane told him. "Sometimes first-round picks don't get signed until the week before the season begins."

Ty couldn't explain why, but news of this delay bothered him, even though Thane didn't seem to mind.

When school had ended, Uncle Gus, still behind in his payments to Lucy, took on even more work. Ty and Charlotte spent their days cleaning a dingy nearby motel. The three long, low buildings lined up along the highway were usually empty during the day, and without air-conditioning the tiny rooms sweltered in the humid summer heat.

Uncle Gus would supervise them from outside, where he'd set up a lawn chair under the shade of a big old oak tree. He kept a small red cooler beside him, sipping down cans of Nestea and listening to WFAN, the big New York sports radio station or, when he could find them, afternoon baseball games. They worked in silence. Although Charlotte was friendly to Ty, she wasn't one for talking, no matter how hard he would try to drum up conversation. When he'd ask her why she didn't like to talk, she'd only shrug, put her iPod earpiece back in, and concentrate on her vacuum.

When they finished cleaning the motel, they'd head for the Breakfast Nook and start right in on all of Uncle Gus's usual clients, six days a week.

By the time Ty got home at midnight, he could only keep his eyes open for two or three pages of his book before he'd conk out for the night. In the morning, they'd have breakfast and start the whole thing over again. On Sundays, they'd go to church and have a decent dinner before Uncle Gus would put on his fishing hat, scoop up his tackle box, pole, and a cooler of beer, and trudge back through the woods to a secret pond he had, for what he called a well-deserved day of rest. Ty would spend Sunday afternoons curled up in the coolest place he could find to catch up on his reading.

They did have one break in this routine. Uncle Gus had a small winning streak betting on baseball games with Lucy and decided to take them all to Atlantic City for two days. While Uncle Gus spent his time in the casino, Ty, Charlotte, and Aunt Virginia got to splash around in an overheated pool laced so strongly with chlorine that Ty had bloodshot eyes for an entire week. For the first time in his life, he couldn't wait for summer to be over so that school could begin.

On August 16, a puddle of vomit greeted Ty in the men's room at Lucy's. He sidestepped it, gagging and trying not to let his mind think about the source of the chunks. He knew from experience that rotten smells would go away after about ten minutes. In science class they called it olfactory extinction. A really bad stink could only go so long before a person's brain just stopped registering it.

Ty knew if he tried to clean the puke first, he'd throw up himself, so he started in on the toilet. He was elbow-deep in toilet water when Uncle Gus banged open the bathroom door, shouting something about Tiger.

Ty peeked out of the stall just in time to see Uncle Gus's foot hit the puke with a slippery squelching sound that sent his feet flying up over his head. The cell phone shot out of his hand, banged into the metal stall, and clattered to the tiles. Down Uncle Gus went, flat on his back in the puddle of vomit.

He rolled, screaming, and got it all over his hands. Some must have gotten in his eye because he pawed at his face, covering it with the slimy stink. He screamed again, until his own retching cut it short. With his head bumped back up against the urinal, Uncle Gus puked on himself before he pulled himself up by the sink and stuck his head under the faucet.

Ty bit hard into his lip. When Uncle Gus finally stopped choking, he raised his dripping head halfway out of the sink, cursed, and stabbed his finger at the phone on the floor.

"Your brother needs to talk to you," he said in a weak voice. "He says it's important."

CHAPTER TWENTY-ONE

"HELLO?" TY SAID.

"What happened?" Thane asked.

"Uncle Gus slipped," Ty said. "He dropped the phone."

"Well, we *signed*," Thane said, his voice verging on a scream from excitement. "Are you sitting down?"

Ty flipped down the toilet seat, backed into the stall, and sat. Uncle Gus wiped his face with a handful of paper towels and scowled.

"Five years," Thane said, almost losing his breath, "*thirty-two million dollars* with a seven-point-five-million-dollar signing bonus. Seven point five million! Today! I'm coming down there to sign it and they'll give me a check! We're rich, Ty! We're really rich!"

• • •

Ty tried to get Aunt Virginia to let him wear the Nike sweat suit Thane bought for him, but she insisted he wear his church clothes along with an old polka-dotted tie from Uncle Gus's closet.

"You don't wear a jogging suit to a five-star restaurant," Aunt Virginia said, primping her hair in the bathroom mirror and tucking it behind her ears.

"Thane won't care," Ty said from the narrow hallway, tugging at the stiff, itchy collar of the dress shirt.

"Well, *I* care," Aunt Virginia said.

Her mouth curled into a snarl, and Ty retreated to the living room, where Charlotte sat on the couch listening to her iPod, the skirts of her pink dress ballooned around her so that she looked like an enormous frosting flower on a birthday cake. Ty sat down beside her. Charlotte looked over at him, then went back to staring straight ahead into space.

"You wonder why I don't talk?" she asked, flicking off her iPod. "This is why."

"What's 'this'?"

"This," she said, puffing the folds of her dress without shifting her vacant stare. "I look ridiculous. When you don't talk, it's easy to pretend that you're invisible."

"That's what you pretend to yourself?" Ty asked.

Charlotte nodded. "It works. After a while people stop trying to talk to you, and after that, they don't even see you. You're invisible, and in this family, that's a good thing to be. With that crazy tie they've got on you, you should try it, too."

Ty looked down, smoothed the red tie with its white polka dots, and heaved a big sigh just as Uncle Gus stormed in from his bedroom, buttoning his shirt cuffs and yelling at Aunt Virginia to hurry up or they'd be late.

"You can't be late for a business dinner," Uncle Gus said, projecting his voice through the wall.

At the sound of the word "business," Ty's stomach got queasy. He wanted to ask Uncle Gus what he meant, but thought he already knew, and realized it wouldn't make any difference anyway. Ty had heard snippets of Uncle Gus's conversations with Aunt Virginia about his bar, the Tiger's Lair, on and off since the NFL draft. Now, with seven and a half million dollars in the bank, Thane wouldn't have the excuse of not wanting to spend money he didn't have. Even though this dinner was supposed to be a contract-signing celebration, Ty feared it would melt down into an argument between Thane and Uncle Gus.

Aunt Virginia emerged in her yellow dress wearing white lace gloves and holding a small matching pocketbook, and they left through the front door, loading up into the truck. Ty got in first and wedged himself into the narrow space behind the front seat. Charlotte sat in between her parents, bobbing her head, listening to her iPod. From where Ty sat, he could see the dark bush of hair sprouting from Uncle Gus's ear. He tried not to look, but his face was so close that he couldn't stop staring. Ty waited until they reached the smooth road of the highway before he cleared his throat and summoned up his courage.

"Uncle Gus?" he said quietly.

"What?"

"I was thinking about the Tiger's Lair," Ty said.

"Or, Tiger's Place," Uncle Gus said. "That's up to him. Just because I like the Tiger's Lair doesn't mean that's what it has to be. When you're partners, you have to work together."

"Maybe tonight isn't such a good time to talk about it, though," Ty said. "I'm just thinking."

"Don't think," Uncle Gus said, "and don't talk. You have no idea about this stuff."

Ty looked to Aunt Virginia for help, but she was picking something out of her teeth and staring intently at the road.

When they arrived at Barelli's, Uncle Gus hopped out and announced to the parking valet that they were there to see Tiger Lewis.

"Is he here yet?" Uncle Gus said, studying the parking lot on the side of the building. "Did he come in a limo?"

The valet shook his head and pointed inside, saying Tiger had arrived ten minutes ago. Uncle Gus cursed and herded them up the stairs and into the restaurant.

The bar was on their right; men in suits and women in fancy dresses sat around it, sipping wine and amber drinks in big teardrop glasses. To the left was the hostess stand and the tables beyond that. Uncle Gus barged past the hostess, waving his arms.

"Tiger! Hey!" Uncle Gus shouted. "You multimillionaire, you!"

In the far corner of the restaurant, by the front window, Thane sat with Morty at a big round table. He wore a black sweat suit like the one Ty wanted to wear, and his face turned red at the sound of their uncle's voice. Every person in the place turned to stare at Uncle Gus, but he seemed not to notice and proceeded across the floor, talking loudly about how lucky the Jets were to have his nephew and how he deserved every bit of his thirty-two-million-dollar contract.

Morty introduced himself, shaking hands with a forced smile. Thane's embarrassment faded, and his own smile grew, when he saw Ty. He stood up and put Ty into a headlock, kissing the top of his head.

To Charlotte, he said, "Wow, look at this pretty girl."

She blushed. Thane sat Ty down in the chair immediately to his right before shaking hands with Uncle Gus and nodding hello to Aunt Virginia.

"Thanks for this iPod, Tiger," Charlotte said, holding up the tiny machine.

"Ty got it for you," Thane said with a grin.

"Time for a drink," Uncle Gus said, sitting down and signaling the waiter by snapping his fingers. "We need to make a toast."

Thane and Morty both said they were fine with sparkling water, but Uncle Gus shrugged and said he'd have a bottle of whatever fancy Italian beer they could come up with fastest.

"When in Italy, drink beer like the Italians," Uncle Gus said, nodding and winking at Morty.

When his beer came, Uncle Gus raised the bottle and said, "A toast to my nephew, a rich man, a football hero, and our success together in business."

Thane nearly choked on his sparkling water. Morty set his drink down and licked his lips, taking a piece of bread and passing the basket before softly asking what business Uncle Gus was referring to.

Uncle Gus swigged his beer before he banged the bottle down on the table. When he spoke, he was impatient and he even sounded angry.

CHAPTER TWENTY-TWO

"THE TIGER'S LAIR," Uncle Gus said.

Aunt Virginia shot him a dark look, and his face and voice softened a bit.

"But we don't have to call it that," he said. "Tiger has to make the call on a lot of this, but the concept is basically a sports bar that Jets fans can go to. He doesn't have to be there all the time or anything."

Thane hung his head and his lower lip disappeared beneath his teeth. Morty puckered his lips. Ty took a piece of bread, biting into the thick, rich crust and handing the basket to Charlotte, who glanced at her father and shook her head apologetically at Ty.

"I mean," Uncle Gus said, talking even faster, "it'll help if he shows up every once in a while, randomly, to keep people guessing on when they might get to bump into him, or some of his teammates. That would be ideal, kind of a Jets hangout where regular people can go. Maybe we even have a Jets night and we charge a cover at the door. I've got plenty of ideas like that.

"We'll make a mint."

"I'll be honest," Morty said. "I don't recommend these things, bars."

"This would be a *sports* bar," Uncle Gus said. He swigged more beer, dampening his thick gray mustache with foam.

"Even sports bars," Morty said, buttering his bread.

"It could be more like a nightclub," Uncle Gus said. "Or a restaurant that has a bar."

"Anything like that," Morty said, setting down his knife. "But you're . . . family, and I understand how that can be."

Uncle Gus smiled big, nodding his head so that a thick tuft of his hair fell in a clump, covering his forehead.

"But you need to know the standard terms," Morty said, pointing at Uncle Gus with his piece of bread. "The way these things work. Tiger gets ten percent of everything."

"Ten?" Uncle Gus said, his smile growing so big that his crooked yellow teeth glowed in the candlelight. "I can do that. To be honest, I thought it'd be more, not that I'm saying I'd do more. Standard terms, you know."

"Ten percent is all you can expect when you're not putting up any of the money," Morty said, biting into the bread.

Uncle Gus looked confused. His mouth began to work itself back and forth underneath the eaves of his mustache.

Before he could say anything, the waiter asked if he could take their order. Ty asked for spaghetti with tomato sauce. When the waiter asked if he'd like something with it, like a veal chop, Ty swallowed and looked at Thane.

"Get it," Thane said. "We're celebrating."

The waiter took everyone's order, and they all sat quietly for a moment before Uncle Gus cleared his throat and asked Morty, "What do you mean Tiger's not putting up any money?"

"He can't," Morty said.

"Why not?" Uncle Gus said. "I'm the one doing all the work. We need three hundred thousand to get started, build out the bar, inventory, kitchen, a big sign. He just puts up the money and watches it grow."

"Maybe we should talk about it another time," Morty said. "You can come into my office and we can go through it all. I'm his financial adviser, so I've got a fiduciary duty. It's not up to Thane."

"It's his money, isn't it?" Uncle Gus said, picking

viciously at the label on his beer bottle.

"Yes, but I'm managing it," Morty said. "It's a good way to do things."

"So I could manage part of it, too," Uncle Gus said. "The sports bar part."

"The NFL Players Association only recommends licensed financial consultants," Morty said.

"Who are you? God or something?" Uncle Gus said in a loud voice. He slammed his hand down on the table, jarring the silverware and drawing the attention of everyone around them.

"Tiger," Uncle Gus said, forcing a smile, "you can *tell* him to do this. It's a *family* business."

Thane held up his hands. "I don't know enough about all this. It's easier just to have Morty do it. I just need to focus on football. I already missed three weeks of camp."

"Actually, he's got to report right away, after this dinner," Morty said.

"What about what I need to do?" Uncle Gus asked. "Who do you think is taking care of—"

Uncle Gus stopped and shot a glance at Ty. Ty's face burned.

Thane glared at their uncle and gripped the edge of the table, his knuckles turning white.

"What does that mean?" Thane said, growling.

"Nothing," Uncle Gus said with a whimper, wiping his mustache on his sleeve.

"Because," Thane said, nearly choking on his words as he looked from Ty to his uncle, then to his aunt, and finally to Morty before the next words burst from his mouth. "Because Ty can come with me."

CHAPTER TWENTY-THREE

"TIGER. EASY, EASY, EASY," Morty said. "He can't go with you. You've got training camp, then the season. He needs a family, your aunt to cook and clean his clothes and all that. You're barely out of college. You're not ready for that. It wouldn't be good for Ty."

Thane clenched his teeth so that his jaw muscles rippled.

"Ty's got nothing to do with this bar business anyway," Morty said to Uncle Gus. "Right?"

"It's just a family thing, that's all," Uncle Gus grumbled, looking into his lap. "You don't even want him helping his family?"

Aunt Virginia put her hand on top of his and gave it a shake, whispering something softly to him. The corners of Uncle Gus's eyes sagged. He looked suddenly tired and sad.

"When someone needs an operation to save their life but they can't afford it," Morty said in a soft voice, "that's when you need to help your family. Believe me, I know."

"I'm sorry," Uncle Gus said, looking up at Thane. "I didn't mean anything by it. I thought it would be good for everybody."

"You'll come to my office," Morty said kindly. "We can talk about it. Let's just have a nice meal. To celebrate. If camp food is as bad as they say, this'll be Tiger's last decent meal for a while."

With his fast talking, and some harmless jokes, Morty had a way of making everyone forget about the discomfort of their conversation about money, and soon the talk turned to Tiger and how many touchdowns he'd score for the team in the upcoming season. Still, Ty kept an eye on his uncle and he could tell that the smile he wore beneath the thick mustache was strained and ready to fall the second they got out the door.

After dinner, on their way out, Thane grabbed Ty and pulled him back into the restaurant.

"You okay?" he asked.

Ty nodded his head. "Don't worry about me."

"Well, I do," Thane said.

"I'm fine."

"You let me know if you're not," Thane said. "I don't care what Morty says."

"Morty's right," Ty said. "I don't want you to end up like the guys who play for ten years and they're broke."

"Not me," Thane said, smiling and tousling Ty's hair.

Thane looked around, then reached into his pocket and took out a hundred-dollar bill and slipped it into Ty's hand.

"Hey, I want you to take this," he said. "In case you ever need something."

"I can't," Ty said, trying to give it back.

"It's just a hundred," Thane said. "Don't insult me."

"I don't want to be a mooch," Ty said.

"What did I tell you about that?" Thane said. "You didn't ask. It'll make me feel better to know you've got something socked away, for an emergency. Don't tell them."

"I won't," Ty said, cramming the bill into the bottom of his pants pocket.

Thane gave him a hug that Ty didn't want to end, but it did when Aunt Virginia stuck her head back inside the restaurant and said they were waiting. Ty bit the inside of his cheek and told his brother good-bye.

When they arrived at Lucy's the next day, they found Mike in the kitchen hunched over a big frying pan of eggs. He grinned so hard when he saw Ty that the end of his cigarette popped up into the air, sprinkling ashes into the pan. Mike squinted at the eggs and tilted the pan toward Ty.

"Looks kind of like pepper, don't it?" Mike asked.

Uncle Gus laughed out loud.

"Hey," Mike said to Ty's uncle, "you want a donut? I can whip some up."

"Great," Uncle Gus said. "Is Lucy in?"

"Check his office," Mike said. "I'll have a batch of powdered sugar ones done before you leave."

Uncle Gus grinned at the big former football player and told Ty and Charlotte to get going. Ty dragged his supplies into the bathroom while Uncle Gus stood outside Lucy's office, quietly knocking on the red door.

Ty filled his bucket, poured in some cleaner, and went right into the stall to get that over with. He was scrubbing the underside of the seat when he caught sight of the rusty air vent from the corner of his eye. He couldn't help wondering what Uncle Gus might be saying to the bar owner. After a quick look at the door, he knelt down in the corner and put his ear to the vent.

Ty heard the sound of Lucy's TV playing. It blurred the words of the conversation, but he could just make them out.

"Stop crying, will you?" Lucy said. "You can't run a bar anyway; you'd drink all the profits. You want to make some extra money? I'll tell you how."

Lucy's voice softened, and Ty could no longer hear

what was being said over the sound of the TV. He
thought he heard Tiger's name once or twice, but he
couldn't be sure. Finally, he gave up and got back to
work. He was scooping cigarette butts out of the urinal when Lucy raised his voice so loud Ty could
almost hear it through the wall. He scrambled back to
his place in the stall.

"Do you know what kind of opportunity this is?"
Lucy said. "Don't worry about the kid. If I ask him,
he'll do it."

Ty's stomach knotted up. Whatever it was they
were going to ask, he didn't want to know, let alone
do whatever it was. The thought of that, or maybe
something else, made him dizzy. He stood up and
stumbled out of the stall, grabbing for the sink to
steady himself.

*Ty and Thane walked out into the dark, snowy
evening, leaving the warmth and popcorn smell of the
movie theater behind for the cold, stiff seats of Thane's
rusty old Subaru wagon. It was the day before
Christmas Eve. Thane was home for the holiday. On
their way out of the theater, an old neighbor who was
a big SU football fan recognized Thane. While Thane
signed a napkin for his son, the man asked if speed
was the thing that made Thane the player that he was.*

*After Thane scraped the car window free from ice
and snow and climbed in next to him, Ty asked, "Why*

did you tell that guy speed wasn't the most important thing? Everyone says that's why you're great but you."

"And what did I say?" Thane asked, blowing into his hands before he started up the car.

"Instincts," Ty said.

"That's right," Thane said, looking over at him with a serious face, "because speed without instincts is useless. When you catch that ball downfield, there are plenty of people trying to knock you out and keep you from the end zone. I can't explain it, but you have to 'feel' where everyone is and in that same instant to know where they're all going to be when they start to chase you. Then your legs have to take you to wherever that opening is, without even thinking about it. That's instinct. It's knowing what to do, where to go, without even thinking."

"How can you know without thinking?" Ty asked.

Thane grinned at him and said, "Trust yourself. If you feel something, follow it. That's instincts. That's what makes a good player great. That's what makes you win."

Uncle Gus banged open the bathroom door, startling Ty from his daydream and sending his heart off on a gallop.

"I wanna talk to you," Uncle Gus said. "Me and Lucy."

Ty knew they were going to ask him for something,

a favor. And he knew he'd have an opening to ask for something back. His instincts told him that.

He only hoped that when he saw Lucy's face and that boiling red scar, he wouldn't be too scared to ask.

CHAPTER TWENTY-FOUR

TY SWALLOWED AND WASHED his hands and followed his uncle out of the bathroom and into the office on the other side of the wall. Sunlight leaked in around the edges of the window's metal blinds. The musty deer head hanging above Lucy's desk stared down at him like an old friend. Opposite the desk, the three-foot plasma TV played highlights on *SportsCenter*. On the wall next to the bookcase filled with DVDs, Ty saw that the calendar had a different woman in a tiny bathing suit than last week. Just beyond that, Ty could see into Lucy's private bathroom with its big glass shower, black marble floors, and fluffy towels. Ty couldn't help wondering if his instincts had been wrong. Maybe they just wanted to talk about the way he cleaned Lucy's private bathroom, too much ammonia smell or not enough sparkle in the gold faucet fixtures.

Lucy had his lips wrapped around a cigar and he squinted at Ty through the smoke. The crowbar lay across his desk.

"Sit down," Lucy said in a tone too pleasant for talking about cleaning a bathroom.

Ty sat in one of the leather chairs facing Lucy's desk, and his uncle took the other one.

"Your brother," Lucy said with a smile, clicking off the TV with his remote and picking up the crowbar, "we're all proud of him."

Ty nodded along with his uncle.

"Your uncle says he's not interested in the bar business," Lucy said. "And that's fine."

Ty relaxed a little.

"But your uncle, like every other red-blooded American," Lucy said, "wants to take advantage of the opportunity that all of a sudden he's got this nephew who's this big football hero and he's playing for the Jets. So, I got an idea that doesn't cost anyone anything."

Uncle Gus nodded his head, smiling hard.

"It's fantasy football," Lucy said, waving the crowbar. "People are crazy for it. It's all for fun, but they pay big money if they can get any edge at all. Injury information. That's a big thing. Stuff the average guy can't get. Stuff he'll pay for."

Lucy raised his eyebrows, but Ty could only shake his head. He knew about fantasy football, getting a bunch of friends and making your own league, picking players all over the NFL for your own team, then assembling a starting roster online. You got points based on each of your individual players' statistics for that week's performance in their *real* game, but Ty didn't get how injury information had anything to do with it.

"Come here," Lucy said, motioning with the crowbar for Ty to come around the desk.

Lucy opened the newspaper to the back of the sports section.

"Injury reports," Lucy said, laying the crowbar down and running his finger along some of the fine print in the box scores. "Who's going to play, who's not? They post these reports even for preseason games. Look, here. Thomas Jones, the Jets running back. It says 'Elbow. Questionable.' Probable means twenty-five percent chance he can't play. Questionable means fifty percent. Doubtful means seventy-five percent chance he won't play. If it says he's out, he won't play at all."

Lucy looked up, and Ty nodded that he understood.

"Good," Lucy said. "But half the time these things are bogus. The team says probable even when they know a guy isn't going to play. Or doubtful when they know he is."

"Why?" Ty asked.

"Strategy," Lucy said. "If the other team knows Jones isn't playing, they know the Jets will have to try and throw the ball more. They can spend more time working on their pass defense. It's a little edge like that that can make the difference in the ball game. For the fantasy players, if they start a guy who's going to be out, they're sunk. Let's say they put a quarterback onto their roster for that week who doesn't even play. It's almost guaranteed that they'll lose. These mokes will pay good money to know who's *really* going to play and who isn't."

"How could I know?" Ty asked.

"You ask your brother," Lucy said, grinning. "You go see him, say, on Friday after school or something and you get the rundown."

"He's going to want to know why," Ty said. "I don't know if he'll like it."

"You just tell him you're in a fantasy league with some of your buddies in school," Lucy said. "Your brother will love it."

"But I can't lie to him," Ty said, seeing the opportunity in Lucy's churning dark eyes. "So, I'll have to just get into a league."

"Yeah," Lucy said, nodding. "You do that, kid."

"Problem is," Ty said, sighing, "the guys who do it are all on the football team. They won't let me in if I'm not on the team."

"So, you'll get on the team," Lucy said, his voice turning into a low growl, obviously annoyed with the details.

Ty looked at his uncle, who nodded so fast that it reminded Ty of a bobble-head.

"That's up to Uncle Gus," Ty said, staring at his uncle.

Uncle Gus's head slowed down, and his eyebrows knit into a V beneath the bulging vein in his forehead.

CHAPTER TWENTY-FIVE

"I'D HAVE TO GO to work late," Ty said, still looking at his uncle. "If I'm going to be on the team."

"So you go to work late," Lucy said, scooping up the crowbar, glaring at Ty, and then at his uncle. "Am I missing something? This is important."

"No," Uncle Gus said, relaxing his face and sniveling to Lucy. "He can do that. He can play."

"Maybe we should have it that I can have dinner with Thane on Friday nights," Ty said. "To get the latest on everyone's injuries."

"Perfect," Lucy said.

Uncle Gus's face contorted, probably at the thought of cleaning his own toilets on Friday nights again.

"Right?" Lucy said to Uncle Gus with that growl of his, pointing the crowbar.

"Uh, yeah," Uncle Gus said.

* * *

That night, as they drove home from their last job, Uncle Gus drank a can of beer and complained through his cigarette smoke about the new arrangement for Ty that would begin in just two weeks. Uncle Gus argued with himself over what had taken place as if Ty and Charlotte weren't even there.

"*I want to be in a fantasy football league,*" Uncle Gus whined in a high-pitched voice, mocking Ty. "*I have to be on the team.*

"I have to listen to that crap?" Uncle Gus asked, looking at his own face in the rearview mirror. "Lucy all of a sudden runs *my* business, too? I don't pay him enough when I bet on the stupid Yankees?

"No, no," he argued, drawing hard on his cigarette and squinting with one eye at the dark road ahead. "This could be big. This could make us a lot of money. Lucy's giving us a chance here. We need to take it. We don't need the kid to get the job done. Besides, he'll only be a couple hours late. Football season doesn't go year-round."

Then Uncle Gus scrunched up his face. He shot an evil look into the mirror and asked, "Who's going to clean the crappers? Who? Huh?"

And so it went, the entire trip home. When they arrived, Uncle Gus shut off the engine. When he opened the truck door, he fell out onto the muddy ground. A stream of curses spewed from his mouth as he struggled to his feet, steadying himself on the hood of the truck, and staggered toward the house. Ty and Charlotte sat still in the cab, waiting for Uncle Gus to get inside before they dared to follow. They knew better than to get in his way after he'd had a few beers.

Charlotte removed the iPod earpieces from her ears. When she spoke, it startled Ty.

"How did you do it?" she asked in a whisper.

"Get it so I can come late and miss Fridays?" Ty asked.

"You're missing Fridays?" Charlotte said, her eyebrows climbing her forehead. "Some partner you are."

"Now we're partners?" Ty said.

"I don't even *talk* to anyone else," Charlotte said, slapping the dashboard.

"Yeah," Ty said, "well, that's not normal."

"What *is* normal about this family?" Charlotte asked, throwing her hands in the air. "The Porta Potti they make you use in the woods? The beer? The gambling? Leaving the windows shut when he smokes those cancer sticks?"

"That doesn't mean you have to clam up."

A strange smile curled the corners of Charlotte's lips and she said, "I got that from your mother."

Ty stiffened and said, "Don't talk about her."

"It's true. That family reunion in the Poconos?" Charlotte said. "I heard her say to your brother, 'If you can't say anything nice, don't say anything at all.'

Well, I'm not saying anything then. You see the crap I have to put up with. What's there to say? Now you're slithering out of it and I'm still stuck."

"I'm not slithering," Ty said. "They've got some fantasy football thing they want me to help with."

"Why can't I help?"

Ty glanced at the front door. Uncle Gus had fallen off the step and was flailing about in the bushes.

"If I could help you, I would," Ty said. "He's not going to go for it and you know it. You should have seen his face when Lucy told him I had to play football."

"Did the vein in the middle of his forehead bulge out all purple?" she asked.

"Kind of."

"Good," she said. "One day maybe it will bust wide open."

"Don't say that," Ty said.

Charlotte snorted and crossed her bony arms like the legs of a spider.

It was Ty's last Friday when he came out of the bathroom at the Nook with a toilet brush in one hand and a bucket in the other and stood face-to-face with a tall blond woman wearing sunglasses.

"I want a bagel," she said, examining the underside of one of her long pink nails.

Uncle Gus had gone across the street for a beer,

and Charlotte was back in the kitchen.

"Uh," Ty said, "this place is closed."

"The door was open," the woman said in a snotty tone. She wore an expensive running suit and shoes. Dark roots shone beneath her long blond hair. Her lipstick matched her nails, and her teeth glowed white in a mean smile. "So just give me a raisin bagel with cream cheese. I'll take a black coffee and an orange juice, and make sure you wash your hands first."

Ty looked at his toilet brush. His cheeks warmed, and the bell on the door behind the woman tinkled.

"Hurry up, Mom," said a voice Ty recognized even before he saw the face. "We're gonna be late."

Then, Calvin West stepped out from behind the woman. His face went blank with shock at the sight of Ty, then his eyes went from the brush, to the bucket, to the bathroom, and back to Ty as his wicked grin grew.

"Hey, Ty Lewis," Calvin said, "cleaning the crappers. You don't want him touching your food. Let's go."

"Be quiet, Calvin. I'm hungry."

Charlotte appeared from the kitchen and stood next to Ty, absorbing the situation.

"I told them the place is closed," Ty told her under his breath.

"I want a raisin bagel," Calvin's mom said. "You don't have to be a Phi Beta Kappa to do that."

Charlotte didn't say anything. She turned and dug

into the big trash can behind the counter, coming up with someone's half-eaten raisin bagel with cream cheese spurting out the side. She plopped it down on a napkin and set it on the counter, then looked up at Calvin's mom with a deadpan face.

"Enjoy," she said.

Then she took Ty's arm and dragged him into the back until they heard the woman utter a curse and then the door jingling as they left.

"That was Calvin West," Ty said, too breathless to appreciate Charlotte's joke.

"Big deal, Calvin West. If he bothers you," she said, putting her earpieces in and picking up a dishcloth, "you let me know."

CHAPTER TWENTY-SIX

THE JETS BROKE TRAINING camp, and the team gave the players the weekend off before the regular season and the real games began. Thane got permission from Uncle Gus to take Ty with him house hunting on Saturday afternoon. He showed up driving a new Escalade. Uncle Gus ran his hands greedily over the shiny black surface of the hood as he admired the machine and told Thane not to bring Ty home too late, as if he really cared.

Inside the truck, Ty gave his brother a kiss on the cheek and a hug. In a whisper he asked if Thane could bring Charlotte, too.

"Yeah, sure," Thane said, and he leaned out his window. "Uncle Gus, can Charlotte come with us?"

Uncle Gus had the garden hose going on a crab apple tree. He stiffened, then a smile grew on his face.

"We can all join you, sure."

"Naw, just the kids," Thane said. "I can't take you guys. I don't want the real estate agent to think I'm some kind of baby who can't pick out his own house."

Uncle Gus didn't get the answer out of his mouth before the front door shot open and Charlotte streaked past him, flung open the back door, and dove into the truck.

"Great," Thane said, and they rumbled away down the rutted track, swishing through the dusty green weeds.

As they pulled out onto the open road, Ty looked back at Charlotte, who smiled so big and so real that she looked like a girl with a storybook life. He winked at her and then rolled down the window and let the wind blow across his face.

They met Linda Roche, Thane's real estate agent, at the highway exit for Summit and followed her Mercedes through a series of twisting roads before they came to a hilly, tree-filled development with houses that rivaled the size of Halpern Middle School. Linda pulled up a driveway and got out in front of a gray stone house with a slate roof.

"There's five garage doors," Charlotte said, blinking and counting them off with a finger.

They got out and followed Linda past the towering columns and in through the front doors.

"You could play football in here," Ty said, his voice echoing off the empty walls and the wood floors.

"It's only eighty-two hundred feet," Linda said to Thane. "At two-seven, it's the best bargain in northern New Jersey. The owner's wife missed her family and they moved back to Brazil."

"Two-seven, as in million?" Ty asked, raising his eyebrows.

"It's an investment," Thane said, stuffing his hands in his pockets and looking around. "Where's the TV room?"

"There's a home theater on the lower level," Linda said, leading them into the spacious, glass-lined back of the house that overlooked an immense grass yard. "Here's the living room. Right off your kitchen so whoever cooks can be involved with whatever's going on."

"So, like, when I put a can of SpaghettiOs in the microwave, I won't miss a single play on *Monday Night Football?*" Thane asked.

Linda looked to see if he was serious and slowly said, "Something like that. The master bedroom is on the first floor."

"That's good," Thane said, following her into the big bedroom overlooking the back lawn and through a maze of closets and the bathroom. "If my knee swells up on me. No stairs."

"Is your knee okay?" Ty asked.

"Yeah, I'm just saying, in case."

"His and hers bathrooms," Linda said, leading them. "Water closets. Walk-in showers. Tub for her. Sauna for you."

"What *her?*" Ty asked, wrinkling his forehead.

Thane frowned and shook his head. "There's no her. Relax."

"Yet," Linda said, raising a finger in the air. "Margery at my office wants your number."

"Yeah, she's cute," Thane said with a nod. "Let's look upstairs."

They followed Linda up the back set of stairs and down a long hallway full of bedrooms.

"I know it's more than you need," Linda said, "but for resale, a house this big needs lots of bedrooms."

"Man," Charlotte said, peering into a bedroom that had its own tiled bathroom. "Ty and I should come live with you."

Ty flashed a scowl at his cousin, forced a laugh, and said, "She's kidding. Kids need a mom, right? Aunt Virginia cooking and cleaning for us. All that stuff."

"Her, clean for *us?*" Charlotte said. "And cooking? We'd do better at McDonald's on a bad day."

"She's kidding," Ty said to his brother, patting him on the back. "We love Aunt Virginia and Uncle Gus. How about those caramel apples she makes?"

Ty wheeled on Charlotte, glowering and holding his finger up to his mouth to be quiet. She shrugged and looked at him like she didn't understand, but she nodded her head anyway.

"Yeah," Thane said, looking up at the vaulted ceilings and studying the chandelier as they wound their way down the big spiral staircase. "I used to complain about our mom's cooking. Remember that goulash stuff with the elbow macaroni?"

Thane stopped at the bottom of the steps, looked up at them, and in a soft voice said, "Then you don't have it and you miss it, even if it was bad. Right, Ty?"

Ty looked at his shoes, and they all stood still for a moment, until Charlotte said, "I didn't mean to—"

Thane waved his hand in the air and started off again. "No, don't worry. It's good to talk about her sometimes, even when we're kidding about her goulash. She'd get a kick out of it."

"What do you think?" Linda asked as they wandered into the kitchen area.

Thane looked around and said, "I'll take it."

"Well, I have a lot of other places," Linda said. "I didn't mean it like that."

"No, I'll take it," Thane said. "Microwave. Home theater. Big shower. That yard is big enough for me to set up a JUGS machine and run patterns. It's perfect."

"I'll draw up the papers," Linda said, the look of shock fading.

"And you two," Thane said, pointing to Ty and Charlotte and then flicking his finger toward the stairs. "Go pick one of those bedrooms. I know you can't move in, but when you come to visit I want you both to have a room. We'll get some furniture and computers and stuff. A couple TVs. Linda, you've got a decorator for me, right? Make sure she talks to the kids."

CHAPTER TWENTY-SEVEN

TY GOT OFF THE bus on the first day of school and hurried to Coach V's office next to the gym. Coach V sat typing on his computer until Ty cleared his throat.

"Hey, Lewis," Coach V said, swiveling around in his squeaky metal chair. "You have a good summer?"

"Yes," Ty said, "and I can play football."

Coach V frowned and said, "What about the family business?"

"My uncle is going to pick me up after he cleans Lucy's," Ty said, and saw the look of confusion on the coach's face. "It's a bar. Kind of a sports bar."

"Oh, well, good," Coach V said, handing him a stapled stack of papers. "Here's the new playbook. You can have the first copy. It's not that much different from the one I gave you in the spring."

"I gave that back to you," Ty said. "Remember?"

"What happened?" Coach V asked. "Your uncle get religion? Figured football would save your soul?"

"Something like that," Ty said. "Well, I gotta get to homeroom."

"Hey, Lewis," Coach V said.

Ty turned around at the door.

"You're in for good this time, right?"

Ty nodded.

"So I'm putting you in as my starting wide receiver, the Z," Coach V said. "I can still see the catch you made in that passing scrimmage."

The coach gave him a thumbs-up and Ty hurried off to his homeroom.

As Ty pushed open the wooden locker room door, he could hear the buzz of his teammates. But as he walked into the throng, it got suddenly quiet and the crowd opened up, making a clear path to the locker he had claimed during gym class. The smirking faces were contagious, and Ty began to smile himself as he approached whatever it was sticking up from the bench in front of his locker. A notebook-paper sign flew like a flag from the top of a wooden handle. Below, the smooth rubber cup of the plunger stood planted on the wooden seat.

The words scrawled on the paper in blue pen came into focus:

TOILET
TY
THE TURD GUY

Ty fought to keep the corners of his mouth up in their smile. He blinked back the tears of shame and bit into his lower lip.

The crowd broke out into an uproar of laughter, punctuated by bursts of glee.

"Toilet man!"

"Come clean my crapper!"

"Toilet cleaner!"

"I heard your job stinks!"

"Toy-tee-Ty!"

"Watch out, don't let him touch you!"

"Turd Man!"

"Wash your hands, Turd Man!"

The locker room door slammed open, smashing into the metal cage and sending a shiver through the room that left it suddenly silent except for Ty's single sniff.

"What's going on?" Coach V asked, glowering. "You sound like a pack of hyenas."

Calvin West stepped from the crowd into the space in front of the plunger, hiding it from Coach V.

"We're excited, Coach," Calvin said, grinning at his teammates, who chuckled nervously. "Lewis gives us that speed in the passing game you're always talking about, right?"

Coach V looked at Calvin sideways and puckered his lips, then nodded and said, "Well, get your gear on and let's get out there."

When the coach walked out of the locker room, the team erupted in nervous laughter. Calvin reached behind him, picked up the plunger, and held it out to Ty.

"Your scepter, O King of the Turds."

A fresh wave of laughter rushed over Ty. He slapped the plunger aside and pushed past Calvin West, opening his locker and focusing on tying the cleats Thane had bought him.

He ignored their words and he ignored their glee, knowing that anything he did would only keep them at it. After a few minutes, even Calvin turned his attention to getting ready for practice. They had plenty of gear to put on: knee, thigh, and hip pads along with a protective cup; rib and shoulder pads along with a helmet up top. Soon the locker room bubbled with the sound of popping snaps, clicking plastic, and players slapping each other's pads.

Ty wriggled into his equipment, then slipped out through the door and onto the practice field. Players clustered like cows in a pasture, one big group and several smaller ones milling about aimlessly, waiting for the coach's signal. Coach V looked at his watch and blew the whistle, yelling at them to all take a lap and then line up for stretching. Ty fell into the slow-moving mass and headed up the sideline. By the time he reached the corner of the end zone, the players had spread out according to their speed, the smaller skill players up front and most of the linemen trailing behind, anchored by Kevin Tully, a two-hundred-and-fifty-pound eighth grader with a bulging gut.

Only a handful of players ran in front of Ty. He bumped up his speed and began to pass them, one by one. Calvin West ran second from the front. Ty hesitated, and Calvin looked back over his shoulder.

"Go ahead," Calvin said, huffing, "pass me, Turd Man."

Ty's brain grew hot and he kicked in a burst of speed, looping around Calvin to the outside, ready to make him look silly.

On his way past, Ty saw Calvin kick out with his right foot. He felt a sharp pain in his ankle, lost his balance, and tumbled toward the ground.

He hit the turf and saw stars. Someone else running past tramped on his hand with their cleats, stumbling into the line and knocking down a bunch of other players. Laughter mixed with grumbles, and from the middle of the field Coach V screamed at them to stop fooling around. Ty got up slow, cradling his aching hand and limping back into the middle of the line, not just humiliated, but hurting.

He didn't think things could get any worse.

He was wrong.

CHAPTER TWENTY-EIGHT

AFTER STRETCHING AND AGILITY drills, Ty followed the other receivers as well as the running backs to a skeleton passing drill where they ran patterns and caught balls thrown to them by the quarterbacks. Ty ran the patterns well but had difficulty hanging on to the passes because of his throbbing hand. That wasn't the bad part.

The bad part came when they began to work on blocking.

"When we run the ball," Coach V said in a voice as rough as broken concrete, "you ladies can't just stand there. Every play, you need to block the defenders downfield, the cornerbacks and safeties. That's why they call them safeties. They're the guys who make the tackle if the runner gets past the linebackers. You don't know which play will be the one where Cooper breaks through. If he does, and you make your blocks downfield, a ten-yard run turns into a touchdown. Understand?"

Ty understood, but knowing something and doing it, especially in football, were two very different things. Coach V put them into a white chalk circle he called "the pit." The wide receivers and defensive backs faced off, one on one, to see which one could smash the other outside of the circle.

When Ty got to the front of the receivers' line, Calvin West pushed his way to the front of the defensive backs' line and entered the circle. Ty got down into a three-point stance, the way he'd seen the other receivers do. Calvin West bent his knees and lowered his shoulder pads, holding his gloved hands out in front of him and flexing them. Coach V blew the whistle. Ty launched forward.

Calvin dipped his head and hit Ty up under the chin, knocking him back. At the same instant, he jammed his hands into Ty's chest, lifting him up and driving him back. Before Ty knew it, he'd been blown outside the circle, but Calvin kept driving him until Ty tripped over a teammate and landed flat on his back with a thud that cost him his breath. Calvin popped up and stood over him, howling with a war cry. Other players hooted and cheered and slapped Calvin on the back, and after his whistle sounded, even Coach V praised Ty's enemy.

"That's the way it's done!" Coach V shouted. "Next two, up!"

The drill kept going and no one paid attention to Ty as he slowly rose to his feet.

At the end of practice the starting offense squared off against the starting defense to scrimmage, the closest thing to a real game the players would get in practice. Ty wanted to impress Coach V, and when the first play called in the huddle was a long pass, he thought he'd get his chance. When he jogged out to the Z position, Calvin West moved directly opposite him, smirking and flexing his fingers.

"Here we go, Turd Man," Calvin said under his breath. "I'm tearing you up twenty-four seven."

Ty thought about the move he'd put on Calvin in the passing scrimmage at the beginning of the summer.

"Bring it," Ty said, lowering his hips and digging his cleats into the turf for good footing.

At the snap of the ball, Ty darted one way, then the other. He flew by Calvin, grinning to himself until he felt something clip the back of his heels. Down he went again. Calvin West stood above him, grinning and bouncing on the balls of his feet until he dashed away.

The whistle blew the play dead. When Ty got flattened, Michael Poyer had thrown a short swing pass to the running back on the other side of the field. Ty struggled to his feet, his head ringing.

"Where were you on the go route, Lewis?" Coach V shouted as he approached the huddle.

"He knocked me down, Coach," Ty said.

"Well, don't let him."

"Didn't you see what he did?" Ty asked.

"You think I've got eleven sets of eyes?" Coach V asked.

"He tripped me," Ty said.

Coach V shot a glance over at the defense. Calvin West held up his hands and shrugged. "Feet got tangled, Coach."

Ty said, "That's not—"

"Enough," Coach V shouted. "Next play. Let's go. We're wasting time. Get out into the pattern, Lewis. All the speed in the world doesn't do any good if you can't get downfield."

Every play Calvin West lined up in front of Ty, and every play he did something cheap: tripping, holding, kicking, even diving at the back of his legs from behind. Calvin knew just when to do his dirty tricks, how not to get caught, and how to make Ty look useless. By the end of practice, Ty had tears of rage in his eyes. He kept lining up, though, telling himself that Calvin would get tired of it sometime, but he never did.

By Friday, a handful of teammates who weren't buddies with Calvin let Ty into their online fantasy league. Charlotte told him he could use the outdated computer in her room. Now he could truthfully ask Thane for the information Lucy and Uncle Gus wanted. Uncle Gus cut the Jets injury report out of the morning paper at the breakfast table and gave it to Ty for a guide.

"You get the real story on these guys," Uncle Gus said. "Especially Jones, the running back. It says he's questionable with a bad knee. That's a fifty percent chance he'll play. We need to know for certain one way or the other."

As far as Ty's real team went, he was ready to quit. Bruises, welts, and swollen knots of flesh covered his legs, arms, and hands. While he caught an occasional pass, more times than not he found himself the subject of Coach V's ranting for not getting downfield into the pass pattern. Only once did Coach V ream out Calvin West for a blatant pass interference, and even then, Calvin didn't seem disturbed. He only nodded his head and put a sorry look on his face that evaporated the instant Coach V turned away.

But the reason Ty thought seriously about quitting before Friday's practice wasn't the bumps and bruises. It was because Thane was going to pick him up from practice to take him to dinner, and Ty was afraid his older brother would see him taking a licking from Calvin West.

As practice progressed, Ty kept an eye on the street. When Thane's Escalade pulled up, Ty's stomach knotted up tight. Thane didn't get out, but the driver's side window rolled down and he smiled and gave Ty a thumbs-up. Ty gave him a quick wave and got back to business.

On passing plays, he used his most elusive moves. On run plays, he hit Calvin as hard as he possibly could, blocking with a ferocity that often kept Calvin away from the play, but never ended without Ty on the receiving end of some kind of cheap shot, often after the whistle had blown the play dead and the contact was supposed to have stopped. Finally, Coach V lined them up for conditioning. In the ten wind sprints across the width of the field, Ty outran everyone. Coach V praised him, but his voice lacked the luster it once had when he talked about Ty's speed.

Ty jogged inside and changed quickly. Thane had rolled up the window to talk on the phone, but when Ty opened the passenger door, he said a quick good-bye and snapped the phone shut.

Thane hugged him and kissed the top of Ty's head. "What do you say? Barelli's?"

"The best sauce I think I ever ate," Ty said, reaching for the stereo controls.

"This Friday night thing is going to work out great," Thane said. "When you're in the NFL, the weekend starts Monday, so it's not like I'm going out on the town or anything on a Friday. It's a good time to catch up. How's school?"

"Same as always," Ty said, turning the music up.

They listened to Everlast until the end of the song, then Thane reached over and turned the volume way down.

"Hey," he said, glancing over. "I want to talk about football."

"You guys are playing the Lions Sunday, right?" Ty asked.

Thane shook his head. "Your football."

Ty looked out the window. "Not much to talk about. I'm learning the plays."

"I'm sitting here, thinking I want to go punch your coach in the face," Thane said, his face tight and turning color.

"What do you mean?" Ty asked.

"Who's that kid?"

CHAPTER TWENTY-NINE

"WHAT KID?" TY ASKED.

"You know. The kid with the cheap shots every play."

"It's football. It's rough, right?" Ty said. "You say that."

"Don't worry," Thane said, glancing over at him. "I'm not going to throttle some twelve-year-old, even though I'd like to, but I want to know what's up." .

"Calvin West. We don't like each other," Ty said, biting into his lower lip and concentrating on the garbage truck ahead of them.

"That crap isn't right," Thane said, "and I'm going to fix it."

"You never had that?" Ty asked. "You told me they were mean to you. Kids. Dumping your books and stuff."

Thane clenched his teeth and nodded. "That's different. That was me."

"Who fixed it for you?" Ty asked.

"Myself."

"So?" Ty said.

Thane stamped on the gas. The big Escalade roared and shot out around the garbage truck, passing it before Thane slowed back down and looked over at Ty. "Then you stalk him."

"What's that?"

"A bully is a bully," Thane said. "In middle school or the NFL. Sometimes a guy's got it in for you, or he wants to make a name. You stalk him. He'll stop."

"But what's *stalking*?"

A mean smile curled up the corners of Thane's lips and his eyes narrowed. "Everywhere he goes? You get him. You don't worry about the play. You hunt him down. You smash him. You chop block him. You leg whip him. If he goes down, you pound him. You never let up. From the snap of the ball to the whistle. It's brutal and it's relentless. That's stalking."

"What if I'm supposed to run a pattern?" Ty asked.

"I didn't see you getting into the pattern out there just now," Thane said. "You fix this first. If you don't, Ty, I will. I'm not going to let that happen to you."

"I'll fix it," Ty said.

"Good."

"Will you show me some things?" Ty asked.

"Sure," Thane said. "We'll go by the facility and I can show you on the blocking dummies. It's on the way to Barelli's anyway."

The Jets' New Jersey training facility was so new that Ty could smell the paint on the walls as they walked down the hallway toward the locker room. Dark green carpet covered the floors. Each wide locker held dozens of pairs of shoes and the player's assemblage of pads as well as his helmet. In front of each one rested a wooden stool. Thane wanted to change into some workout clothes to show Ty his tricks, so they stopped at his locker. Quiet filled the vast room, but on the far wall Ty could see through the glass partition into a room full of equipment where a handful of players rested on tables.

"What's that?" he asked.

"Training room," Thane said, pulling on a pair of shorts and sitting down to lace up a pair of cleats he'd removed from the bottom of his locker.

"What are they training for?" Ty asked.

"No," Thane said with a small laugh. "They're hurt. Injured guys getting treatment from the team trainers. Trying to get better."

The image of Lucy flashed into Ty's mind, and he asked, "Is Jones in there?"

"I doubt it," Thane said, craning his neck and peering into the room.

"I read he was hurt," Ty said.

Thane snorted and waved his hand in the air. "He's fine."

"So, he'll play?"

"For sure," Thane said. "He's a little bruised up, that's all. He'll take some aspirin."

"Otherwise, he'd be in here now?" Ty asked.

"You got it. When you're hurt, your only job is to get well," Thane said, glancing into the room. "A couple of those guys are on Injured Reserve, out for the season. They got hurt in training camp. The others are trying to get ready for the Lions."

"And they have to stay here?" Ty asked.

"The trainers will work with these guys almost twenty-four hours a day to get them back on the field," Thane said. "There's all kinds of things you can do. Ice. Ultrasound. Electronic stimulation. Stuff that helps speed up the healing process. It works, too. You want to see?"

"Sure," Ty said.

Thane tied his shoes tight and led Ty across the locker room and into the training room. A dozen padded tables lined each wall. At one end, stainless steel tubs rested alongside a bubbling tile hot tub big enough for twenty people. At the other end, the trainers' offices stood beside a doctor's examination room that had its own X-ray machine. Some players sat on their tables loaded down with ice bags on their necks, shoulders, knees, or ankles, their bare feet sticking out from under white towels. Others lay on their stomachs with rubber pads stuck to their limbs and wires running between the pads and small machines that looked like mini-microwaves on wheels.

Most of the players wore headsets and bobbed their heads to music. One had a book, and Ty asked Thane his name.

"Conrad Rommel," Thane said. "Meanest offensive lineman in the game. He likes Charles Dickens. *A Tale of Two Cities* and stuff."

"The guys don't give him crap?" Ty asked, staring across the locker room at the enormous player.

Rommel had a nose like a small lightbulb and a soft round face with a little smile. His tufted brown hair was nearly gone, and except for the barrel chest and arms that looked like gallon jugs of milk, he might have been an English teacher or an accountant.

"He's pretty mean," Thane said.

"He looks nice."

"Oh, he's nice off the field," Thane said, and as if to prove it he waved. "Hey, Conrad."

Conrad looked up from a frayed paperback book, adjusted his towel, and grinned at Thane, waving back before he returned to his book.

"The best players are," Thane said. "But when they play, they flip the switch."

"Flip the switch?"

"Mad-dog mean," Thane said. "That's how you've got to play. Everyone gets mad—it's just what you do with it. The meanest players store it up. Someone cuts them off in traffic, they smile. Neighbor's dog craps on his lawn? No big deal. Hubcaps get stolen? You get some more.

"Yeah, but then they get out onto the field and it all comes out. They flip the switch and, man, are they mean."

"Are you?" Ty asked.

Thane smiled at him and angled his head toward the door. "Some people say that. Come on, I'll show you some tricks and then you can flip the switch on that goofball Calvin Weasel."

"It's Calvin West."

"Calvin the Weasel to me."

"You really have tricks?" Ty asked.

"And they never fail. Come on. You'll see."

CHAPTER THIRTY

A BAND OF ORANGE glowed beneath the dark clouds over the far end of the practice fields. The scent of grass floated on a small breeze. The blue blocking dummies stood rigid and waiting like a row of perfect soldiers beneath one of the goalposts. Thane ambled up to the middle one and crouched down into his stance.

"The most important thing? Stay low," he said, then fired out, smacking the dummy with both hands, driving it so far back that the metal arm holding it disappeared into its piston and clanged like a bell.

"Wow," Ty said.

"You always have to have your pads lower than his," Thane said, softly karate-chopping the dummy to show Ty where to hit. "Low man wins. Your helmet, under his. Your shoulder pads, under his. The aim point for your hands is right here, in his chest. Try it."

"I don't have cleats or anything," Ty said.

"Don't worry. Just get a feel for it. Keep your head up and try to have your forehead hit him in the neck at the same time you strike with your hands."

"I thought you block with your shoulder," Ty said.

"That's the trick," Thane said. "Most receivers, they block with their shoulders. But if you watch the good linemen in the NFL, at a big college program? It's hat and hands."

"Hat?"

"Your helmet. The old-school coaches, they call it a hat."

"You hit with your helmet?" Ty asked.

"And keep your head up. Bull your neck."

Ty got into a stance and fired out, striking the bag with his hands and bumping his forehead on the pad. He saw stars, and the dummy rattled but barely moved.

"Not bad. Now, the other trick," Thane said, standing beside the next dummy in line and jabbing his finger into its chest. "You don't aim for here with your hands. You aim for here."

Thane waved his hand behind the dummy and patted the connection bar in the middle of its back.

"You don't explode *into* the man," he said. "You explode *through* him. Like he's made of Jell-O and you want your hands to make contact with his spine."

"Kind of gross."

"Mad-dog mean," Thane said, "that's what you've got to be."

Ty worked at it until the orange in the sky faded to deep purple, banging away at the dummy, staying low, firing through, hat and hands. Thane coached him on little details like taking a shorter first step, popping his hips, and grabbing his opponent's jersey after the initial hit.

"They'll never call holding if you keep your hands inside," Thane said, gripping Ty's T-shirt at the seam just in front of his armpits. "All this stuff is legal. You explode into the Weasel, get a grip on his jersey, and drive him all over the field. If he goes down, you get up quick and go at him again."

"When he's down?" Ty asked.

"If the whistle hasn't blown?" Thane said with a crooked grin. "Bam. Right down on him. Full force. You drive him into the dirt."

Ty took a deep breath and nodded.

"It's all legal," Thane said. "The real tough guys? They don't have to cheat. They get it done before the whistle."

"I've blocked him, you know."

"I saw. Listen, you might not get him the first time," Thane said. "You might not get him the second time. But football's about—"

"Getting up," Ty said. "Keep going."

"He'll stop his crap," Thane said.

"What about after the whistle? What if he cheap shots me then?" Ty asked.

Thane shrugged and said, "Then you fight him. You hit him openhanded, right in the ear hole. That'll send a shock wave through him. Don't use a closed fist or you'll break your hand. But that's only if he starts it. If he does, then finish it. It's part of practice, not like punching someone in a game. You never do that."

Ty frowned but nodded his head that he understood.

Thane smiled at him and messed up his hair. "Don't worry. You'll be fine. Let's go get some veal chops."

"And apple crisp," Ty said, following his big brother, bouncing on his toes from excitement over his new football tricks and the thought of the delicious meal to come.

"With ice cream," Thane said.

"Two scoops," Ty said.

"Three."

They both laughed and went inside to the locker room so Thane could change back into his clothes. While he did that, Ty eyed the players in the training room, searching without success for even a hint of meanness in Conrad Rommel's face.

When their apple crisps were reduced to a sprinkling of crumbs in shallow puddles of melted ice cream, Ty took Uncle Gus's injury list from his pocket and smoothed it out on the tablecloth.

"What you got?" Thane asked, wiping his mouth on a napkin and leaning back in his chair.

"I'm in this fantasy league," Ty said, concentrating on the paper, afraid that if he looked his brother in the eye that Thane would see right through the scam. "With the guys on my team. What I wanted to ask was if you'd give me the deal on these guys. My whole team is mostly Jets players, and those are the guys I want to put on my roster."

"'Cause we love the Jets."

"Yeah," Ty said, "but if these guys aren't going to play against the Lions, I'd hate to put them in my fantasy lineup. And if, like, Kerry Rhodes isn't playing, I don't want to use the Jets' defense. They're not that good on D without him."

Thane scowled and leaned forward, scooping up the paper.

"Hey," he said. "Where'd you get this?"

CHAPTER THIRTY-ONE

"NEWSPAPER." TY SAID.

Thane's frown grew into a smile as he looked at it. He leaned back.

"Yeah, sure," he said. "I'd go with our defense all the way. Rhodes? He'll play. He was the guy in there getting the electronic stim on his lower back."

"How come it says 'doubtful' for him then?" Ty said, eyeing the scrap of paper. "That's, like, a seventy-five percent chance he *won't* play."

"A lot of guys wouldn't," Thane said. "A back like that? Spasms? That's bad stuff, but he'll medicate it and go."

"Medicate? What do you mean?" Ty asked, thinking of the cough syrup his mom used to give him.

Thane gave him a crooked smile and said, "A shot.

Novocain. Medicine. They'll numb it up."

"A shot in his back?" Ty said, shuddering.

"Rough way to make a living, huh?" Thane said. "That's why you make sure you study hard. Be a doctor or something. Here, let me see that thing."

Thane went through the rest of the list, giving Ty exactly what he knew his uncle and Lucy wanted; then Thane paid the check and took him to the mall, where they caught a horror flick. Thane bought two big buckets of popcorn and sodas the size of small lampshades. When Ty got home, he hugged his brother and kissed him good night on the cheek.

"Fun, huh?" Thane said, patting Ty's leg.

"Awesome," Ty said. "Hey, good luck out in Detroit."

"Next week we're home and you're coming to the game, right?"

"Absolutely," Ty said. "And I'll see you Friday night again, too?"

"It's our night, my man," Thane said. "I'll see you then."

"Did you get it?"

Ty woke up to the smell of beer and pickled eggs and cigarettes. Like a dark cloud, Uncle Gus blocked out the thin yellow light that normally leaked into the laundry room from the kitchen. His stubby hands gripped Ty by the shirtsleeves, lifting him off the battered mattress on the floor.

The words stuck in Ty's throat, and Uncle Gus shook him.

"Did you get it? Jones? Is he hurt? What about the others? What about Rhodes?"

"I'll tell you," Ty said, coughing. "Can I get a drink?"

Uncle Gus squinted at him, then cursed under his breath, dropping Ty to the mattress and stumbling into the kitchen. Ty got out of bed and felt the cold linoleum beneath his feet. He tottered into the kitchen, rubbing the sleep from his eyes. Uncle Gus shoved a glass of water at him, sloshing it all over Ty's pajamas. Ty took a drink, and Uncle Gus slapped another copy of the injury report down on the kitchen table, rattling the top to the sugar bowl.

"Tell me," he said.

Ty bent over the piece of paper and went down through the list, telling Uncle Gus everything that Thane had given him. When he finished, he looked up and saw Uncle Gus's yellow teeth glowing at him in the weak light from above the stove.

"That's good," he said, punching a number into his cell phone. "Lucy? It's me, Gus. Yeah, I got it. Yeah it's good. Really good."

Uncle Gus threw open the refrigerator door and snatched a can of beer from the top shelf, popping it open with a hiss. Ty backed into the laundry room. He lay down on his mattress in the narrow space between the washing machine and the wall, pulling the thin covers all the way up over his head and holding them tight over his ears so he didn't have to listen.

When they returned home from church on Sunday, Ty chopped wood until Aunt Virginia called him in for Sunday dinner at noon. He and Charlotte—who also wanted to see Thane—cleaned the dishes as fast as they could while Aunt Virginia went shopping and Uncle Gus settled down in his chair with a can of beer. Ty darted into the living room still drying his hands on a dish towel as the Lions kicked off to the Jets.

After two running plays, Thane caught a seventeen-yard pass across the middle and took a massive hit from a Lions defender. He held on to the ball, though, and the Jets drove down the field with Thomas Jones running strong and Thane catching another ten-yard pass to set up a field goal.

Uncle Gus scooped his cell phone off the little stand beside his chair. "Lucy? How about that?"

Uncle Gus listened, then furrowed his brow and said, "I know it's only three nothing, but the spread's two so we're already in the catbird seat, right?"

Uncle Gus listened some more, then frowned and closed his phone before looking up at Ty and asking, "What are you looking at?"

"Nothing," Ty said.

"That's right," Uncle Gus said. "Let's see how Rhodes plays before we get excited."

"Okay," Ty said.

Rhodes played well, leading the Jets' defense in shutting down the Lions almost completely. Thane caught a forty-two-yard touchdown pass on the next series, and Uncle Gus jumped up and hugged Ty, who jumped up and down with him.

"We're gonna be *rich*," Uncle Gus said. "This is so good."

It didn't stop there. The Jets continued to dominate the game. Thane had 172 yards receiving and added two more touchdowns. Thomas Jones ran for more than a hundred yards, and Rhodes and the defense only gave up two field goals.

One TV shot showed Thane on the sideline celebrating with Chad Pennington and Laveranues Coles. Thane had his helmet off and was wearing a green Jets cap backward on his head. He hugged Pennington, the quarterback, and pointed at him, shouting, "The man," and then they all laughed. The TV announcers talked on and on about Thane—they called him Tiger—and how he'd made as big an opening debut as they could remember for a rookie in his first NFL game.

Uncle Gus's cell phone rang late in the fourth quarter. He knocked over the six empty beer cans on his stand but grinned nevertheless when he put the phone to his ear. He nodded, stroked his big, thick mustache over and over, and said, "I know" almost a dozen times, then hung up and looked at Ty and Charlotte with glassy eyes.

"Five thousand dollars. You hear that? Charlotte, go get me another beer. We keep going like this and I'll show that rat agent of your brother's. I'll open that bar on my own!"

It sounded like a lot of money just to help someone win a couple fantasy games, but nothing surprised Ty anymore when it came to Uncle Gus.

CHAPTER THIRTY-TWO

ON MONDAY, TY WAITED until his teammates emptied out onto the practice field before he removed the plunger from the metal door of his locker. He didn't want anyone to hear the sucking pop it made when he yanked it free. With everyone around, he had pretended it didn't exist. On his way out, he tossed the plunger behind an old set of lockers near the door, then jogged across the wet field just as Coach V sounded his whistle.

Rain poured down in sheets, and the wind whipped spray through the metal face mask and into Ty's eyes. Five minutes into stretching, his practice uniform already clung to his skin, sending shivers through his bones. At the whistle, Ty lined up with the other receivers to run pass routes for the quarterbacks.

Calvin West jumped in front of Ty, grinning through the wet. His blond hair hung like dark seaweed, plastered across his forehead.

Ty crouched down in his stance, digging his cleats into the soggy turf.

"Gonna punk you out, Toilet Boy," Calvin said under his breath, flexing his fingers as a giggle leaked from his throat.

Michael Poyer called out the cadence through the hissing rain and hiked the ball.

Ty took one short, quick power step. He exploded up into Calvin, striking him under the chin with his helmet and in the chest with his hands. He drove his feet. His fingers clawed into Calvin's armpits, digging up jersey and skin so that the tall blond tyrant let out a squeal. Ty kept going, driving him up the field until he tripped and flopped to his back. Calvin flapped his arms and legs like a hurt bird. Ty rose up off of him and blasted him again.

"Hey!" Calvin cried out.

"Lewis!" Coach V screamed, blowing his whistle and running over. "We're running pass patterns!"

Ty looked innocently at the coach, unable to see his eyes behind the water-spotted mirror sunglasses.

"Sorry, Coach," Ty said, holding out his hands. "I thought you said we were blocking."

Coach V frowned and walked away, and Ty jogged to the back of the line.

The next time Ty's turn came up, Calvin let

another defensive back work against him. Ty ran a perfect post route, catching the ball for a touchdown. He wondered if it could really be that easy. It wasn't. The next time, Calvin pushed in front of another player to face off with Ty. Calvin didn't say anything; he simply glared. Ty crouched down in his stance again. Instead of running a deep route straight down the field, Ty blasted Calvin, driving him right past the sideline and over the top of a bench.

"Lewis!" Coach V screamed again. "*What* are you doing?"

Calvin lay moaning on the ground, grabbing at his back with his legs slung over the seat of the over-turned bench. Ty got up and walked away.

"He was pressing me, Coach," Ty said. "I couldn't get him off me, so I figured I should block him. Like in a game."

"In a game?" Coach V said, twisting his face.

"Yeah, that's what you said," Ty said. "If we can't get off a press and the ball gets thrown, make sure we block downfield. We can spring the other receivers for a touchdown that way. That's what you said, right?"

"This is a passing drill," Coach V said, pushing past Ty, kneeling beside Calvin, and helping him up. "Run the pattern."

Calvin sniffled, rubbing his back where it had hit the bench. Ty nodded and turned away before he let himself break out into a grin. Calvin stayed away from Ty during the skeleton pass drill called seven-on-seven and he lined up on the other side of the field when it came to team self-scrimmage as well. But Ty remembered his brother's advice about stalking and being relentless.

On the first play, a run, Ty crossed the entire field on a full sprint and plunged the forehead of his helmet into Calvin's ear hole, dropping him in his muddy tracks as if he'd been hit by a bus. Instead of walking away, Ty reared back and dove on top of him again, pummeling Calvin with all the force he could bring to bear and knocking the wind out of him in a great gasping gust.

Calvin's eyes got big, and his mouth worked open and closed like a gurgling frog. He clutched his neck and rolled his head side to side. Finally, his breath came back in a terrific sob. Calvin's eyes filled with tears. He rolled on his side and threw up what looked to Ty like the remains of a bologna sandwich but smelled of Doritos.

Coach V and his assistant picked Calvin up under the arms and half dragged, half carried him off the field, to the bench, where they sat him down. Coach V patted Calvin's back, then marched out onto the field and blew the whistle, yelling at them to get back in the huddle and stop staring like a bunch of Girl Scouts at a cookie sale.

In the huddle, Ty noticed his teammates glancing at him from behind the bars of their masks. No one said anything, but when he stepped into his place, the players on either side made plenty of room. Poyer winked at him and called an 819 boot pass. That meant Ty would run a nine, just a straight sprint, right to the end zone.

"I'll be open," Ty said.

"I know," the quarterback said.

The cornerback in front of Ty tried to jam him at the line. Ty feinted left, then right, then came back to the left and sped up the field by himself. The pass flew into the air, apparently too far for Ty to get it. He found that other gear and kicked it in with a burst of liquid speed. He stretched and leaned and plucked the ball from the air. His teammates cheered. When he returned to the huddle, everyone clapped him on the back.

That was only the beginning. The rest of that chilly wet afternoon, Ty put on a clinic of running and catching. He couldn't see Coach V's eyes, but Ty had to imagine that they sparkled with joy.

The success of the offense left the team in a festive mood, even during wind sprints. As they jogged to the locker room, no fewer than a dozen players patted Ty on the back. He nearly forgot about Calvin West.

He remembered clearly, though, when Coach V appeared at the entrance to the locker room with a scowl on his face. His sunglasses hung limp from his hands, and his hair dripped rain down his face. His eyes showed no expression, but the tone of his voice sounded serious and angry when he said, "Lewis. In my office. Now."

CHAPTER THIRTY-THREE

TY PASSED THROUGH HIS half-naked teammates and the smell of sweat and mud. His cleats clacked on the tile floor, a lonely sound that echoed off the shower walls. A locker creaked and quietly closed. Through the glass window, Ty could see into the office. Coach V sat with his arms folded, his back to the locker room. The bald spot in the middle of his otherwise thick black hair glowed red. Ty looked back to see everyone staring at him. He offered up a brave smile and turned the corner into Coach V's office.

"Shut the door," Coach V said.

Ty's hand trembled as he reached for the wooden door. He closed it softly until he heard a click.

Coach V stood, leaning toward Ty, hovering over him. His hands tightened into fists, and he banged one of them against the file cabinet. Ty winced at the crash.

"Do you know what you did?" Coach V yelled, his face turning purple. "Calvin West is *hurt*. *Injured*. Out for I don't know how long! What you did was bull! I won't have it! I won't accept it!"

Coach V banged the file cabinet again. Beyond him, through the glass, dozens of frightened faces stared. Coach V spun around, saw them too, and dropped the blinds, cutting off half the light in the office. Ty felt trapped. The walls seemed to close in. Coach V stopped huffing. He grew quiet and sat on the edge of his desk.

When his shoulders began to shake with a chuckle, Ty thought the coach was losing his mind. His mouth turned up at the corners and that scared Ty even more.

"Now, you want to know what I really think?" Coach V said in a whisper, leaning forward and touching Ty on the shoulder. "I think you did good. I think you did *great*. I saw what he was doing to you, but I wanted to see what you were made of. What you did today, *that's* what it takes. Toughness, meanness. You can't just run fast. You gotta have some of that nasty inside you or you get eaten alive in this game. You've got it."

Ty took a deep breath and let it out in a ragged puff. "Why did you yell?"

Coach V glanced over his shoulder at the blinds. Keeping his voice low, he said, "Knocking him over the bench? I can't openly condone that. I'd lose my job. I had to yell at you or I'd have the parents and the principal down my throat. I gotta make it look good. But I'm telling you, man-to-man, what you did, he deserved. You're gonna be a good one, Lewis. Maybe a great one. Now get out of here, and look upset when you leave. This stays between me and you, but if that jerk starts up with you again, you do just what you did."

"You think he'll start again?" Ty asked.

Coach V puckered his lips. "Not openly, but he'll do something. Something sneaky. I'm not worried about out on the practice field, but don't you let him trick you into a fight in school. He's, like, a black belt in Tae Kwon Do or something. And you'll get kicked off the team if you fight, and I need you. You watch your back."

CHAPTER THIRTY-FOUR

THE NEXT DAY, CHARLOTTE found Ty in the corner of the lunchroom, at a table by himself, facing the rest of the cafeteria.

"Want company?" she asked, sitting down and opening up her Garfield lunch box.

"Sure," Ty said. "Why do you still have that lunch box?"

"You think my parents would buy me anything new?"

Ty nodded with understanding.

"Why are you here in the corner?" she asked, picking the salami out of her sandwich and dangling in front of her mouth before slurping it down.

"I don't want Calvin West sneaking up on me," Ty said.

"I heard about that," she said. "Michael Poyer was

talking to someone about you dissing him and him wanting paybacks."

"Coach V told me to watch my back," Ty said, chewing on his peanut butter sandwich as he scanned the lunchroom.

"I got your back," Charlotte said.

Ty looked at her and saw that she was serious.

"You're a girl," he said.

"I'm a year older than him," she said, sitting up straight and drawing her shoulders back.

"Okay," Ty said, not wanting to argue and sorry that he might have insulted her. "Thanks."

Their conversation turned to Thane and his new house and the neat things they thought they'd find in the rooms earmarked for them. After a few minutes, Ty grew quiet.

"What's wrong?" Charlotte asked.

"I just don't want to be a mooch," he said. "You don't think I'm talking like a mooch, do you?"

"You're just excited," she said. "Me too. It's not like we asked for the stuff, but if he wants to do it, all we're doing is being grateful. He wants us to be excited. He's like that, your brother. You are so lucky."

Ty thought about his parents, but he forced a smile and agreed with Charlotte that he was lucky and that Thane was the best. Charlotte looked at her watch and said she'd better go. She had music and the class was on the far side of the school. She patted Ty's shoulder and told him she'd see him after his practice.

Ty watched her go, then scanned the lunchroom before darting to the exit and hurrying down the hall.

He climbed a crowded staircase toward his locker on the second floor. He needed to pick up his science book and folder for his next class. The buzz of conversation stopped when he reached the top landing. The crowd parted, and the traffic on the stairs behind him came to a stop. Calvin West and his three biggest buddies blocked the doorway leading out of the stairwell.

Calvin stepped into the empty space between them, holding his hands in loose fists, up and ready. The stairs behind Ty and the landing below quickly emptied, but beyond that, the packed-in group of faces stared up with wild-eyed excitement.

"Come on, Lewis," Calvin said. "You think you're so tough?"

Ty shook his head. "I don't."

"Don't what, Turd Man? You don't think you're tough?" Calvin said, raising his voice. "You were tough yesterday when you took a cheap shot at me."

"I didn't," Ty said, his voice sounding small and weak.

"I say you did," Calvin said, talking even louder. He stood toe-to-toe with Ty now, bumping his chest into Ty's. "So let's see how tough you really are."

"I don't want to fight," Ty said.

"You little pansy. You're fighting. Right here, right now."

"I don't want to get in trouble," Ty said.

"Boo hoo," Calvin said, whining. "Toilet Turd Face."

"Hey!" someone shouted.

Calvin's three friends turned and pushed at someone who pushed them right back until she burst into the open space on the landing.

"You leave him alone."

"Charlotte," Ty said.

Charlotte had her books under one arm. In her other hand she still carried her lunch box. Pink blotches highlighted the pale moon of her face.

"Wow, Super Freak Girl wants to save Turd Boy," Calvin said, laughing. "You're such a pansy you've got some dorky girl trying to save you. You think you're a football player? You're so weak."

"I said, leave him *alone*," Charlotte said, her voice rising to a scream.

"What are you gonna do, freak?" Calvin said.

He spun around and dumped Charlotte's books, spilling them across the floor.

"You jerk!" she yelled, closing the gap so that her nose almost touched his.

Calvin palmed Charlotte's face with his hand and shoved her backward into his three buddies. They pushed Charlotte back out onto the landing, laughing. But instead of taking it, Charlotte swung her metal lunch box with blinding speed in a wide arc that connected with the side of Calvin West's head with a hollow metal bang.

Every kid in the stairwell sucked his or her breath in at the same time. Calvin's eyes rolled and he staggered like a loopy boxer. Charlotte wasn't finished.

With a high-pitched screech, she grabbed him by the shirt and shoved him, hard. Back he went, stumbling and flying off balance down the stairs. Calvin did a cartwheel and hit the lower landing with a terrific crack and a scream of his own. Charlotte stood at the top of the steps huffing and puffing and glaring down at Calvin, whose arm stuck out from under his body at a funny angle.

"I told you," she yelled over the sound of Calvin's screams. "Leave him alone!"

CHAPTER THIRTY-FIVE

TY SAT NEXT TO Charlotte just outside the principal's office. Through the window they could hear the roar of the ambulance's engine as it pulled away from the school, and then its siren when it reached the first intersection. Charlotte had her arms folded tightly across her chest. She scowled straight ahead, as if daring someone to even talk to her.

The principal's secretary occasionally looked up from her typing to make sure they hadn't escaped. Every couple minutes a teacher would peek inside the door, look at the two of them, shake his or her head, and leave. Ty heard the broken muffler on Uncle Gus's truck from quite a distance. Charlotte's face had shown very little sign of life, but at the sound of her father's truck, she began to breathe in little huffs through her nose.

The rumbling noise came closer and closer, then stopped right outside the window before going quiet. Ty couldn't see from where he sat, but he had a good idea of what Uncle Gus's face must look like: scrunched up tight, swollen, and boiling from red to purple. A minute later, when the office door swung open and that's exactly what Uncle Gus looked like, Ty couldn't help nodding his head.

But Uncle Gus surprised him when he didn't say a word.

Instead, Uncle Gus looked over his shoulder, and Ty saw Aunt Virginia bringing up the rear. She looked like a wet hornet, partially because her hair looked like she'd just gotten out of the shower, but mostly because of the way her eyes had been reduced to pinpricks, so tiny were they behind the big, thick glasses.

"Where is Mr. Clemons?" Aunt Virginia said, puffing up her chest and snarling at the secretary. "I want to know *exactly* what happened here."

The secretary rose from her seat and hurried over to the principal's door, cracking it open and whispering before she turned to face Aunt Virginia.

"Mr. Clemons will be with you in a moment," she said. "He's talking with the other boy's parents. *He's* on his way to the hospital."

At this news, all three adults swung their heads in the direction of Ty and Charlotte to stare. Ty shrugged his shoulders and shook his head.

"Charlotte," Aunt Virginia said, casting a dark look

at Ty, "I can't believe you let yourself get involved. I'm surprised at you."

Charlotte popped out of her seat like a jack-in-the-box.

"You leave him alone!" she shrieked, pointing at her mother. "Ty didn't do anything! All of you, just leave him alone!"

Just as suddenly, she was back in her chair, staring intently at the wall as though she hadn't said a word, huffing through her nose.

"Well," Aunt Virginia said with a gasp. "We'll see what the truth is."

Mr. Clemons emerged with dark, slicked-back hair and a suit that glimmered when the light hit it just right. His fingernails gleamed with polish and a gold watch flashed on his wrist. He spoke with a Boston accent.

"Mr. and Mrs. Slatz?" he said.

"I want to know what happened," Aunt Virginia said.

"We have a conference room right here," the principal said with a slight bow and an open hand extended toward the door.

"Let's go," he said to Ty and Charlotte.

They followed the adults into the room and sat down at the long, dark table under the watchful eye of George Washington. Mr. Clemons folded his hands, resting them on the table.

"Evidently," he said, "this began yesterday in football practice. Ty apparently got a little rough with Calvin West. He knocked him over a bench, right off the field."

Uncle Gus gave Ty a funny, half-smiling look.

"Today, after lunch, in the stairwell," the principal said, "they had words and Charlotte and Ty attacked him. They knocked him down the stairs. His arm is broken and he has a concussion. The parents want us to bring in the police and file charges."

"It's a lie!" Ty said, jumping up. "He hit her. He grabbed her face and shoved her and dumped her books."

"He what?" Uncle Gus said, pounding a fist on the table.

Mr. Clemons held up his hands. "We're getting several versions of this."

"Charlotte doesn't lie," Aunt Virginia said, slapping her palm on the table with a crack that silenced them all. "Charlotte, what happened?"

"I already—" the principal said.

"No," Aunt Virginia said, glaring and slapping her palm down again. "You let my daughter tell what happened. I want to know."

Mr. Clemons swallowed and gave his head a short nod.

"Charlotte?" Aunt Virginia said.

Charlotte kept her arms crossed. She stared at the

table, cleared her throat, and said, "Calvin West was bragging to people that he was going to use his Tae Kwon Do on Ty and beat him up for what Ty did in football practice. When I saw the crowd at the stairs and people were saying 'fight,' I pushed through Calvin's friends and saw him and Ty. Ty said he didn't want to fight and I said for Calvin to leave him alone. That's when Calvin dumped my books and grabbed my face."

"Is that what those red marks are?" Aunt Virginia said, her voice raising to a hysterical pitch.

Charlotte touched the two small welts on her cheek and nodded.

"Then they pushed me from behind, his friends," Charlotte said, looking up with tears in her eyes. "And I . . . I swung my lunch pail and hit him with it and then I pushed him and he fell. Ty didn't do anything. He didn't touch anyone, so why can't everyone just leave him alone?"

Charlotte heaved a sob, then covered her face with the crook of one elbow while she continued to hug herself with the other arm.

"Did you hear *that*?" Aunt Virginia said with a shriek, standing and pointing at Charlotte. "I'm the one pressing charges. This Calvin West, grabbing her face. Look at those marks!"

Mr. Clemons breathed in deep through his nose, held up his hands for calm, and said, "There are several versions of the story. I'm afraid I'm going to have to suspend both Ty and Charlotte from school until we get this sorted out, and I can't rule out expulsion."

"Can I still play football?" Ty heard himself say.

The adults all stared at him.

The principal said, "Of course you can't."

CHAPTER THIRTY-SIX

"YOU JUST HOLD IT right there," Aunt Virginia said, standing up and pointing at the principal.

"Suspend?" she said, arching her eyebrows all the way above her big, round glasses. "Did you say 'suspend'?"

"The boy has a broken arm," Mr. Clemons said in a mutter.

Aunt Virginia narrowed her left eye and tilted her head as if to bring it even closer to the principal. "And he didn't ask for it?"

Mr. Clemons frowned and cleared his throat. "No one asks to be thrown down the stairs, Mrs. Slatz."

"You do that to my little girl's face, you better believe you're asking to be thrown down a flight of stairs, Mr. Clemons," Aunt Virginia said, stabbing a thick finger at Charlotte. "Look at those welts! That's self-defense!

And if you think you're suspending my children for this—either one of them—then you better also believe you'll be hearing from our lawyer, because we will not only sue this school, we'll sue you personally."

The principal opened his mouth, then closed it for a moment before he said, "I know you're upset, and that you probably don't realize what you're saying, Mrs. Slatz."

"Before my carpal tunnel," Aunt Virginia said, flexing her fingers, "I was a paralegal at Price, Meese, and Breen for seven years, Mr. Clemons. So I know exactly what I'm talking about. We sued the Port Authority over a dozen times, and who do you think wrote the complaints? Don't you make the mistake of underestimating *me*."

Uncle Gus clamped his mouth tight under his mustache and nodded his head in total agreement. Ty watched the principal attempt to digest the situation. A greenish color crept onto his face, and a bead of sweat trickled down his forehead. He licked his lips as his eyes darted back and forth between Aunt Virginia and Uncle Gus.

"All right," he said, laying his hands flat on the table. "I'll reserve my judgment until I have a better handle on this."

"You be careful what you do," Aunt Virginia, said, glowering. "A person is innocent until proven guilty. *Proven*."

The clock on the wall ticked away another minute.

Ty felt his question building up inside him like a burp he couldn't suppress. Finally, it came.

"So, I *can* play?" he said quietly.

They all turned to stare at him again with their mouths hanging open. Ty stared back until the principal nodded, then sighed and looked out the window. All the while, Charlotte cried quietly, but this news seemed to cheer her up, because after the principal's nod, she wiped her eyes and sniffed and offered Ty a small smile.

Ty returned to his classes amid whispers and secretive stares. He concentrated on his schoolwork and pretended not to notice. When he arrived at the locker room after the final bell, he noticed right away—no toilet plunger. In the area around him, players laced up shoes and tightened the straps to their pads, stealing looks at him without offering any comments. When Ty walked through the tight space between lockers toward the outside door, teammates he normally had to push his way past stepped back, sucking in their guts and kicking aside loose equipment to make way.

When he emerged into the afternoon sunshine, Ty felt the fresh air and something else lift him so that his shoes barely seemed to touch the grass as he loped off toward the practice field. He caught some passes to help Michael Poyer warm up his arm, then jogged to the center of the field along with the rest of the team at the sound of Coach V's whistle.

"Take a knee," the coach said, an unusual way for him to begin practice.

Coach V whipped off his mirrored glasses and looked around.

"Team," he said. "Team is everything. It's how you win. Wars or football games. Anything."

Coach V began to pace, holding his sunglasses behind his back and clasping his hands there. "Like brothers, sometimes teammates fight."

Ty's stomach tightened. He looked around and swallowed.

Coach V stopped and said, "But we're still a family, a team. We get over it. Now, I know all about Lewis and West. Well, it's over. We're a team. We put it behind us so we can win. Lewis is with us. West isn't. That's life. I don't want it talked about. I don't want it whispered about. I don't want it thought about. Your job, as football players, is to think about football and winning. You treat every man on this team like he's your brother. Period. Everyone got that?"

The team answered with a ragtag collection of yeses. Coach V glowered and growled.

"You got that?" he shouted.

"Yes, Coach!" came the cry in unison.

"Good," Coach V said. "Now give me that first team offense against the first team defense. We're going to scrimmage."

The players cheered, none louder than Ty. Scrimmaging captured the thrill of a game without the pressure, and it beat the pants off the same old drills they usually had to endure at the beginning of practice. Ty dashed into the huddle and listened eagerly as Poyer called a pass play that would send him on a post route, running straight up the field and then heading toward the middle at a forty-five-degree angle.

They broke the huddle and Ty jogged out to the edge of the field, lining up with one foot behind the other at the line of scrimmage, ready to run. The cornerback, Calvin West's backup, eyed him nervously and stiffly got into position in front of Ty. At the snap of the ball, Ty exploded off the line, making the cornerback wince in preparation for an impact that never came. At the last instant, Ty dodged the defender and launched himself up the field, sprinting ten yards before lowering his hips and shooting off to the inside on the perfect angle. He streaked past the free safety, reached out, grabbed the ball, and dashed into the end zone.

The rest of practice was more of the same, and Coach V couldn't keep the gleam out of his eye at the end of practice when he removed his glasses for the second time that day and talked to them about their opening game against their archrival, Brookfield Middle.

"Poyer," Coach V said, "you take care of that arm, and Lewis, you take care of those hands, and we are going to wipe the field with them."

Ty couldn't wait.

CHAPTER THIRTY-SEVEN

TY LOOKED IN THE mirror, spinning his green Jets cap around backward just the way he'd seen Thane do on TV. He smoothed out the sleeve of the sweat suit Thane had bought him and walked slowly out of the locker room, trading nods and slapping high fives with Michael Poyer and a couple of the offensive linemen on his way. Outside, he sprinted across the grass and jumped into Thane's Escalade, which had appeared toward the end of practice. Thane grabbed him and hugged him tight.

"Now, that's the way to practice," he said, whipping off the Jets hat and messing Ty's hair. "You looked like an Edinger."

"Edinger?" Ty said.

"Mom was an Edinger," Thane said, starting up the truck.

"What's Mom got to do with it?" Ty asked.

"How do you think you got that fast?" Thane said, pulling away from the curb. "She took second in the NCAAs in the hundred meter. You didn't know that?"

Ty shook his head.

"She had a brother who played tailback at Alabama," Thane said. "They said he would've been in the NFL but he broke his neck—not paralyzed, but he couldn't play anymore."

"A brother?"

"Younger brother," Thane said.

"How come I never heard of him?"

"They weren't real close," Thane said. "Mom was a lot older. Then they stopped talking. I guess about the time you were born. He did something. They got into a big fight, and she never talked about him again. I asked at Christmas one time and the look she gave me? I never asked again, and then I kind of forgot. He was in Chicago last I knew."

Ty looked out the window. For some reason, learning that his mom had a brother he never even knew about made the empty space inside him seem even bigger.

He didn't want to think about it, so he said, "One week till the opener. Coach says with my hands we can beat Brookfield Middle. They're our archrival. My hands and Michael Poyer's arm, he says. Like you and Pennington against the Bengals, right?"

A wave of pain passed over Thane's face.

"What's wrong?" Ty asked.

Thane shook his head and rolled his eyes. "You're not going to believe it. I twisted my dang knee."

"Your bad one?" Ty asked.

Thane nodded and patted the leg of his sweatpants. Ty heard the crunch and noticed for the first time the lumpy bag of ice beneath the stretchy material.

"Today," Thane said. "In a stupid two-minute drill at the end of practice."

"Man," Ty said.

"I know it," Thane said, massaging his knee through the ice bag. "I already had an MRI. There's no new tear in the cartilage, so that's good."

"Do you have to get treatment?" Ty asked.

"I thought I'd pick you up, go back for some electronic stim," Thane said, "then we could go to Barelli's right from there. It'll only take forty minutes or so."

"Are you gonna play?" Ty asked.

Thane glanced at him. "Why? For your fantasy team?"

"No," Ty said, shaking his head hard. "Just for you. Last week was so awesome. You'd tear that Cincinnati secondary to pieces."

Thane rubbed the back of his neck, steering with one hand, and said, "I guess if I were you, I'd take me off your fantasy team for the Bengals game."

"You're really not going to play?"

CHAPTER THIRTY-EIGHT

"I CAN'T SEE PLAYING this Sunday," Thane said. "This thing is killing me. I know how it gets. It'll take a few days."

Ty felt the injury list in his pants pocket. He didn't even want to ask about the other players now. They rode in silence for a while.

"Don't be so down," Thane said. "I'll be back."

"I'm okay," Ty said.

"You look like you want to ask me something," Thane said as they pulled past the guard shack and into the Jets' facility.

"No," Ty said. "I'm okay."

Ty followed Thane as he hobbled out of his truck, through the locker room, and up onto one of the tables in the training room. Ty counted nine other players in the room. One of them had his back to Ty, listening to his Walkman as he sat on the edge of a cold tub, dangling his ankle in the frigid water. When he finished, dried his leg, and turned around, Ty recognized Laveranues Coles.

"Laveranues," Ty said quietly to Thane.

"Want to meet him?" Thane asked.

Coles headed their way, bobbing to the music. Ty nodded. Thane and Coles slapped hands, and Thane motioned for the other receiver to take off his headset.

"Hey, LC," Thane said. "My little brother."

"Hey, little brother," Coles said, grinning big, slapping his hand into Ty's, and shaking it hard. "You helping my man get well?"

Ty could only nod.

"Good," Coles said. "Give me some of your magic, too, for this ankle of mine, okay?"

Ty kept nodding and Coles laughed and limped off.

"The paper said he's questionable," Ty said, feeling inside his pants pocket for the scrap of newspaper Uncle Gus had given him. "If you're both out, who are they going to throw to?"

"Maybe the tight end," Thane said. "Don't worry. It's a long season."

One of the trainers came over. She had Thane lie on his back before she elevated a section of the table, raising his leg. She connected rubber pads and wires to the stim machine and got it started before pulling a yellow rubber sleeve over Thane's leg.

"What's that?" Ty asked.

"The boot," Thane said as the trainer connected a hose to the boot, bent down, and flipped on what sounded like a vacuum cleaner.

The boot inflated like a rubber raft, then hissed as it deflated, before starting all over again.

"The pressure forces the swelling down," the trainer said. "You all set?"

"I was going to take my little brother here to dinner when I'm done," Thane said. "Am I finished after this?"

"Just make sure you ice down when you get home and be back at six in the morning," she said.

Thane nodded and she left them.

At Barelli's, they ate a dish of sausage, peppers, and chicken that tasted better than anything Ty had ever eaten. But when the apple crisp came, it didn't seem as sweet as it had the week before, maybe because he felt bad about Thane's injury, or maybe because he didn't know how he'd answer Uncle Gus when he asked for a complete injury update. With Thane worried about his own injury, Ty just couldn't start quizzing him about the other players. It didn't seem right.

He wanted to make up his own assessments based on what he'd seen in the training room, but he knew he couldn't lie. Uncle Gus would sniff him out right away. Whenever he lied, his face turned beet red and he began to sweat. Pinocchio had a better chance of getting away with a lie than he did.

No, he'd have to tell Uncle Gus the truth.

All the way home, Ty prayed Uncle Gus had had too many beers and fallen asleep. But when they pulled down the bumpy road and the yellow rectangle of the front window came into sight, Ty could see Uncle Gus's shadow behind the curtain, peeking out, and waiting for him.

CHAPTER THIRTY-NINE

THE MOMENT TY GOT inside the door, Uncle Gus grabbed him by the front of his sweat jacket and pulled him close. Ty could smell the beer, the cigarettes, and the hint of hot dogs with sauerkraut. A mustard stain on Uncle Gus's gray mustache had caked itself into a brownish crud that matched the edges of his teeth.

"I'm sorry, Uncle Gus," Ty said.

"Sorry for what?"

"I couldn't get it," Ty said.

"The injuries?"

Ty watched the look in Uncle Gus's eyes grow wild. His hands began to shake Ty as he dragged him across the floor and tossed him onto the couch.

"Do you know what he'll do?" Uncle Gus yelled. "He'll

break my legs with that crowbar, that's what he'll do."

"Lucy?"

"I told you who he is, what he does," Uncle Gus bellowed, pacing the small space in front of the coffee table. "I *never* should have agreed to this. I told your aunt you were a mistake from the start."

In a quavering voice, Ty explained why he couldn't get what Lucy wanted.

Uncle Gus froze.

"*Tiger's* hurt?" he said in a whisper. "He wasn't in the paper."

"I know," Ty said. "It was late today. It's his bad knee. He doesn't think he can play."

"Not play?" Uncle Gus said, his mouth popping open, the bags under his eyes weighing heavy enough to expose their red rims.

"Laveranues Coles either," Ty said, happy to end Uncle Gus's tirade.

"*What?*" Uncle Gus said, his bloodshot eyes bugging out of his head.

"He was limping through the training room," Ty said. "Thane said they'd have to throw to the tight end."

"No one else knows this," Uncle Gus said, stroking his mustache and turning away, pacing the room and talking to himself as if Ty weren't there. "Without a passing game, Cincinnati should win. The spread is eight. Even if they don't win, Cincinnati's defense will keep it close. The Jets will be lucky to pass for a hundred yards all day without Tiger and Coles. I've got to tell Lucy."

Uncle Gus fished in his pants pocket until he came up with his cell phone. He dialed, still pacing the rug.

"Lucy? It's me, Gus." Uncle Gus listened for a moment before saying, "I got something even better. Tiger's hurt. He probably won't play. *No one* knows. It looks like Coles is out too."

Uncle Gus nodded his head. Ty could hear Lucy's voice leaking from the phone, and even though he couldn't hear the actual words, he could hear Lucy's excitement.

"Yeah," Uncle Gus said, "I got the kid right here."

Lucy said something.

"It's a little late," Gus said, "but sure, okay. I can bring him."

Lucy said something that made Uncle Gus's face lose its color.

"Mr. D'Amico, the boss?" Uncle Gus said, swallowing the word as if it were a chicken bone going down sideways. "Are you sure?"

Uncle Gus nodded and closed his phone. His hand trembled as he replaced it in his pants pocket. His hand came back out, jangling his truck keys. "We're gonna take a little ride."

CHAPTER FORTY

UNCLE GUS GRABBED A fresh can of beer from the refrigerator before leading Ty out to the truck. When they
got to Lucy's Bar, they drove right past. Ty began to
ask why, but thought better of it and bit his tongue.
Uncle Gus didn't stop until they reached downtown
Newark. He pulled up in front of a crumbling brick
building just up the street from the river. Ty hopped
down and stepped into the empty street. A paper cup,
a newspaper, and a swirl of grit twirled past on the
back of a little wind devil. At the corner, a bum
slumped against a garbage can that overflowed onto
the sidewalk.

Ty looked up at the building. A dead pig hung in the
window, dripping blood into a bed of shaved ice. On one
side of the pig hung three dead rabbits still wearing

their fur. On the other side, a row of empty hooks grinned like the teeth of a monster. A TV satellite dish hung from one of the dirty rectangular windows above. The number on the door was "37," with the seven hanging upside down from one nail. The green and red neon sign said, LUDI'S MEATS.

Uncle Gus plunged through the door and started up a narrow set of stairs. Ty hesitated, staring into the butcher shop, where two men with bloody aprons made ringing sounds as they sharpened their knives. One of the men looked up and grinned at Ty with shiny white teeth. Ty jumped and hurried up the stairs after his uncle. When they reached the second-floor landing, Uncle Gus rapped his knuckles softly on the door. It opened a crack, then swung wide, releasing a cloud of cigar smoke into the hallway.

Uncle Gus grabbed Ty by the arm and led him in. Around a big oak table, eight men sat staring suspiciously at each other through the smoke as they cupped their playing cards. At one end of the room, a TV sat on a table by the window. At the other end a stuffed deer head with one antler rested above the fireplace, staring blankly at a battered refrigerator. Each man had an ashtray and his own stack of money on the red and white checkered tablecloth, but in the middle, a messy pile of twenty- and hundred-dollar bills grew beneath a low-hanging light. Finally, the big fat man facing the door slapped down a bill, leaned back in his chair, and said, "Call."

The big man wore a shiny black sweat suit with a tank top underneath. Something bulged underneath his arm, maybe a gun. Thick black hair covered the back of his hands and neck. He began a low, steady laugh that shook his gut. The other players slapped down their cards and groaned at the sight of the big man's kings while he raked in the mountain of cash.

When the big man's eyes flickered over Ty, his laughter went dead. The others turned to see. That's when Ty realized that Lucy had been sitting with his back to them, not realizing he and Uncle Gus had entered the room. The raspberry scar flashed like a bicycle reflector as Lucy jumped up and spun around. He put a long, bony arm around Ty's shoulder and led him toward the table. The men frowned and wrinkled their brows with uncertainty.

"That the kid?" the big man asked.

"My nephew, Mr. D'Amico," Uncle Gus said, wringing his hands. "Tiger's little brother."

The big man, D'Amico, hardly glanced at Uncle Gus before turning his attention to Lucy.

"Well?" he asked.

Lucy faced Ty.

"Tell us about your brother's knee," Lucy said in a sweet but oily tone.

Ty shrugged and repeated everything he'd seen and heard, sick to his stomach at the way they all leered when they heard Thane's name.

"You guys are using this for fantasy stuff, right?" Ty asked.

"Sure, kid," Lucy said.

"And what about Coles?" D'Amico rumbled, scooping up the deck of cards and snapping through them to break the deck so that he could shuffle. "He hurt, too?"

Ty nodded.

"How bad?"

"Thane, my brother," Ty said, the words spilling out of him even though something inside said to be quiet, "he said Laveraneus won't play."

D'Amico snapped the cards down on the checkered tabletop, shuffled them, and grinned, nodding. "You want a sausage sandwich or something, kid?"

Ty shook his head. His stomach turned at the thought of the dead pig hanging downstairs in the window.

"I can't offer you a beer, but you did good," D'Amico said before he turned his attention to Uncle Gus. "You're the uncle?"

Uncle Gus clasped his hands together, nodding wildly.

"Well, you take good care of him," D'Amico said in a quiet voice that scared Ty more than if he'd yelled. "You remember Man o' War?"

Uncle Gus stared, working his lips with no sound coming out.

"The racehorse," Lucy said.

"Yeah, that," Uncle Gus said. "I remember."

"I never lost a bet on that horse," D'Amico said. "I made a lot of money on that horse. It made me real happy."

The big man began dealing the cards, flicking them across the tabletop, a small wheezing sound coming from his chubby lips. When he finished, he narrowed his eyes at Uncle Gus. "I had a feeling when I saw that horse, a good feeling, like he was gonna do good things for me.

"And I get the same thing when I look at this kid."

CHAPTER FORTY-ONE

TY HAD PRACTICE THE next morning, and Coach V asked him what his problem was.

"I don't feel so good," Ty said.

"Yeah," Coach V said. "You look a little pale."

Uncle Gus picked him up from practice with Charlotte. At the donut shop, Ty cleaned the bathroom, then helped Charlotte in the kitchen. Uncle Gus sat at the counter, eating a donut as he dug through a stack of papers and entered figures into a notebook. Ty began to mop the floor behind the counter as Charlotte took the trash out back to the Dumpster.

"You know what I'm doing?" Uncle Gus asked him, a gleam in his eye.

Ty shook his head.

"Figuring how much money I can get my hands on," Uncle Gus said with a wink. He bit into the donut, leaving a blob of jelly and some powdered sugar on his mustache as he chewed. "I'm gonna bet it all. Every cent. Something like this? It doesn't come around too often. The planets are all lined up on this one with the point spread at eight. Why do you look like you ate a bad piece of fish?"

"Fish?"

"Something rotten," Uncle Gus said. "You're all green."

Ty's mop slowed to a stop. "I thought it was all fantasy football. That's what you said."

"So?" Uncle Gus said, lowering his voice to a whisper and leaning toward Ty. "You gotta grab life by the horns. You get an opportunity like this? You take it. Everyone does. Presidents. Rappers. Movie stars. Even your brother. They all catch a break and they take it. This is my break."

"It's gambling, right, Uncle Gus?"

"Not illegal," Uncle Gus said in a harsh whisper. "You can bet in Vegas. Atlantic City. We're not getting into any trouble."

"But it's not right," Ty said.

Uncle Gus widened his eyes and smiled before he let a gust of air blow out from under his mustache, rousting up a tiny cloud of powdered sugar. "Don't be a *fool*."

* * *

Sunday morning, Ty woke to the sound of Uncle Gus's voice on the phone. He gripped the covers and pulled them tight, then rolled over until his nose touched the cool surface of the washing machine.

"Yeah, fifteen thousand," Uncle Gus said, his voice seeping in from the kitchen. "What do you mean? That's everything I've got. Trust me, I wish I had more. I thought maybe you could loan me ten."

Uncle Gus harrumphed, leading Ty to believe the person on the other end of the phone didn't want to lend him the money.

"Yeah, well, just remember," Uncle Gus said in a mutter. "What goes around comes around."

Ty heard the kitchen phone slammed down onto its hook, leaving a little ring in the air. Ty picked up the clock he kept next to him on the floor and saw that it was nearly time for him to go. He slipped out from under the covers and tipped his mattress up against the wall. From the milk crate where he kept his clothes, he removed the Nike sweat suit Thane had bought for him and pulled it on, along with his Pro Shock sneakers.

When he peered around the corner, Uncle Gus looked up from the kitchen table, where he'd spread his papers out underneath a steaming mug of coffee.

"What do you think your brother would say if I asked him for a loan?" Uncle Gus said, taking a sip of coffee and considering Ty over the rim of his mug. "A small one."

Ty felt his stomach tighten. He took a box of corn-flakes out of the cupboard, filled a bowl, and got out the milk. He sat down at the table, as far from Uncle Gus as he could.

"He'll probably say to ask Morty," Ty said, studying the cereal.

Uncle Gus slapped his palm on the table. Ty jumped.

"That's what I thought," Uncle Gus said. "But this is a sure thing. I can't tell him that, but it is. I could make so much money for him, for all of us."

Ty wolfed down his cereal and wiped his mouth with a napkin from the dispenser Uncle Gus had stolen from the Breakfast Nook.

"Thane's funny about money," he said.

"He can afford to be funny," Uncle Gus said. "He didn't get an extra mouth to feed dumped on him when things were tight already."

Ty got up and put the milk away before he washed off his bowl in the sink. "I could ask him for some money for my food. I'm sure he'd do that."

"*Money for food. Money for food,*" Uncle Gus sang in a mocking tone. "That's all you can say? A lot of people are going to get rich on this game today and I want to be one of them."

A horn sounded from out front.

"That's him," Ty said, drying the last bit of his bowl, putting it away, and running for the door.

Uncle Gus followed him. When Ty tore open the front door, Thane was already standing there.

"You didn't have to get out," Ty said. "Your knee."

Thane flexed his leg up and down. "Man, it feels a lot better."

A little choking sound escaped Uncle Gus's throat, and Ty turned to see that he'd lost all his color.

"You're hurt, right?" Uncle Gus said.

"I'm a lot better," Thane said, smiling.

"But you can't play today, can you?" Uncle Gus said, ending his sentence with a squeak and grabbing hold of the door frame to steady himself.

Thane massaged his knee, considering it for a moment before he shrugged and said, "Doubt it. They don't want to take a chance. We've got two divisional games coming up, Miami and Buffalo, and they want me ready for them."

Uncle Gus sighed and let go of the door frame.

"That's smart," he said. "You have to be careful. Uh, Tiger, I wanted to ask you something."

Thane put a hand on Ty's shoulder. "Okay."

"If I have a business proposal," Uncle Gus said, fidgeting with his stubby fingers, "I need to talk to Morty, right? I mean, that's still the protocol?"

"Yeah," Thane said.

"Okay," Uncle Gus said, nodding and holding up his hands in surrender. "That's what I thought. I got something that's like an immediate opportunity, a can't-miss thing, actually. No time to get with Morty on this one, so I thought I'd just check."

Thane stared at their uncle for a minute, then said, "Okay, well, I gotta go. See you after the game."

Uncle Gus clamped his mouth tight and nodded as he watched them go.

When they reached the highway, Ty said, "Sorry about that."

Thane waved him off. "Don't worry. I get stuff like that all the time. I can handle it. Here, look at this."

Thane fished his hand into the compartment between the seats and came up with a glimmering emerald card with letters embossed in silver. It said: JETS VS. BENGALS, and below that: OFFICIAL, and below that: ALL ACCESS INCLUDING LOCKER ROOM.

"What?" Ty said.

"Your pass," Thane said. "You're with me today."

"Even in the locker room?" Ty asked.

"Everywhere," Thane said. "You know that HBO show they have?"

"*Inside the NFL?*" Ty asked.

"This is the *real Inside the NFL.*"

CHAPTER FORTY-TWO

THANE GOT WAVED THROUGH several sets of parking attendants, security guards, and police. They drove down into the tunnel underneath the Meadowlands stadium, where they parked in a row of cars and trucks gleaming with chrome grilles, rims, hood ornaments, and shiny new colors. There were Mercedes sedans and trucks, Porsches, Lexuses, Maseratis, a Bentley, several Ford pickups, and a dozen Cadillac SUVs. Ty's mouth hung open.

He got down and let Thane put an arm around his shoulder, leading him into the concrete guts of the stadium, down a curved tunnel, and past two New Jersey state policemen. Thane pulled open a red metal door with a warning sign on it saying: AUTHO-RIZED PERSONNEL ONLY.

"Us, huh?" Ty said, feeling for the pass that hung from the zipper on his pants pocket.

"Sure," Thane said with a chuckle. "You're with me."

They passed through a short white cinder-block hallway and into the vast locker room. Players milled about, some half naked, some already wearing their football pants stuffed with thigh and knee pads. Most had headsets on and listened to iPods, lost in their own worlds of thought and music as they went about the ritual of taping their joints and dressing for the game.

"I gotta go see the trainers," Thane said, offering Ty the stool in front of his own locker.

"Can I come?" Ty asked.

Thane winced, then said, "Okay."

Ty followed his brother through the pack of enormous men with muscles so big they seemed to stretch skin to its breaking point. One player had laid his entire uniform out in front of his locker, as if whoever had been wearing it had vanished into thin air, leaving only his clothes behind. Ty watched as he started with the socks and began dressing himself from bottom to top.

Looking back like that, Ty bumped into the leg of a giant. He stared up at the biggest human he'd ever seen, bigger even than Mike from Lucy's and certainly in better shape.

"Hey, little guy," the man said in a booming but pleasant voice.

"AC," Thane said, coming back to retrieve Ty. "My little brother. Ty, Anthony Clement."

Ty swallowed and said hello. The giant flashed a set of white teeth, winked, and moved on toward his locker, wrapping one of his wrists with tape.

"He's *huge*," Ty said as he and Thane passed by the tiled bathroom sinks and into the training room.

"Probably the biggest man in the NFL," Thane said. "He's six foot eight and goes about three seventy after dinner. And he's not just big, he can move. That's the thing about the big guys in this league. Even the sloppy-looking guys with the big guts? Most of them can dunk a basketball. How'd you like to have him blocking down on you?"

Ty shuddered and followed Thane into the training room, a less fancy space than what they had at the practice facility. Players sat on the padded tables, not for treatment, but for taping. Half a dozen trainers wrapped ankles, wrists, knees, and elbows with roll after roll of white athletic tape, filling the room with the sound of hissing and snapping as they unwound the tape, wrapped on layer upon layer, and tore off the ends.

In the back, a white curtain blocked off two other tables. A huge offensive lineman emerged from one, rubbing a spot on his shoulder and loosening the joint by rotating it around. Ty saw a tiny spot of blood on his bare skin. Behind him, the doctor tossed a needle into a red plastic waste bin before looking up at Thane and nodding his head.

"How you feeling, Tiger?" the doctor asked.

"Better," Thane said, climbing up onto the table and introducing Dr. Garret to Ty.

Ty shook the doctor's hand as he pulled the curtain shut. He watched as Dr. Garret probed Thane's swollen knee, his fingers sinking into the puffy flesh as if it were a water balloon.

"You're moving better," Dr. Garret said as he poked. "You did a good job with the ice."

"I feel better."

"Let's get this fluid off and you should be ready to go for next week."

"I could go now," Thane said.

The doctor looked up at him and smiled. "We talked about that. The coaches know you'd go out there, and believe me, everyone appreciates your mind-set. But it's a long season, and it's early. Let's get this thing under control. We can win this without you, right?"

"I hope so," Thane said.

The doctor lifted an enormous needle from his table of instruments. The cylinder looked like a breakfast juice glass, and the needle reminded Ty of a small drinking straw. Dr. Garret swabbed the side of Thane's kneecap with alcohol and poised the needle before looking at Ty.

"You might want to step outside," Dr. Garret said to him.

"You gonna put that under his kneecap?" Ty asked, swallowing the acid and cornflakes churning up from his stomach.

"That's where the fluid is," Dr. Garret said. "He'll be okay. You wait out there."

CHAPTER FORTY-THREE

TY LOOKED AT THANE, who nodded and did his best to smile. Ty slipped outside the curtain, his hands gripped tight and sweating as he listened. He heard the doctor say he was sorry in a low tone, and he heard Thane suck air in through his mouth and the creak of the table.

When Dr. Garret whipped open the curtain, Thane sat clutching a cotton swab to his knee. As the doctor dropped the syringe into the bin, Ty saw the yellow fluid that filled the cylinder and its swirling crimson cloud of blood. Thane hopped down and limped out, grabbing Ty by the shoulder and using him like a cane. One of the team's smaller players, a defensive back with tattoos covering his muscular torso, walked past them and into the doctor's area. Ty heard the curtain slide closed.

Thane greeted his teammates, wishing them luck, slapping high fives, and introducing Ty as they moved through the locker room. When they got to his locker, Thane gave Ty a big green Jets sweatshirt and a white cap with the green logo and told him to put them on.

"This is great," Ty said, admiring the thick logo patched across his chest. "Thanks. I'll give it back after the game."

"Take it home," Thane said as he changed into his own sweatshirt, pants, and hat. "Free stuff is good for you."

Outside the locker room, they wound through the tunnel and out onto the field. White clouds filled the sky, with only a random patch of blue or an occasional shaft of sunlight gleaming through. The small breeze hinted at autumn and carried with it the scent of hot dogs and barbecue.

The stadium buzzed with excitement as the stands filled up with green-and-white-clad fans. A handful of fans hung out over the tunnel entrance above them, screaming Tiger's name and begging for autographs. Ty looked up at them. Several had painted their faces green. Thane took their footballs, hats, and programs, signing them with a flourish until the yelling died down.

Players in full pads and uniforms jogged, huffing, past them and out onto the field, where they began to bang into each other and warm up their legs. Thane led Ty to the bench. They sat down, and Thane put his arm around Ty's shoulder. Behind them, and beyond the bench area outside a thick yellow line, TV and newspaper reporters and VIPs milled about like a tightly packed school of guppies.

Thane flexed his leg, gripping his knee.

"You okay?" Ty asked, nervous to see a TV camera pointed their way, its red light glowing like a demon's eye.

Thane nodded.

"That was nasty," Ty said. "All that gunk in your knee, that huge needle. That had to kill."

"It's a rough way to make a living, my friend," Thane said. "But that's why we get the big bucks. Don't think about it. Enjoy the game. Enjoy just being here."

Ty nodded and turned his attention to the field.

The Bengals players covered one end of the field, and the Jets took the other. In the middle, on the fifty-yard line, several pairs met, shaking hands, trading hugs, and chatting.

"What are they doing?" Ty asked. "Aren't they supposed to be getting ready to knock each other's lights out?"

"Lots of guys know each other from college or from playing on the same team in the NFL," Thane said. "Some of them from off-season charity events. Most guys in the league are friends with one another. It's like a fraternity, a club."

"Some club where you smash each other's brains in," Ty said. "Coach says Brookfield is, like, the enemy."

"The Bengals are, too," Thane said. "But only during the game."

"That's kind of weird."

"But it works," Thane said. "Come on, everyone's going to be going back inside before kickoff. Let's see what the coach has to say."

Together, they walked down the sideline and into the tunnel. Before they got too far, the team came streaming past, and they stood back as the players and coaches poured into the locker room. By the time they followed, the team had already circled up around the coach, most of them down on one knee while some stood. The fiery words washed over Ty. The energy inside the locker room and the blazing eyes of the massive players glazed in sweat made his hair stand on end. He found himself thinking about what would happen if the Jets won big.

Uncle Gus, Ty knew, would be ruined. And if the confidence in the coach's voice and the looks in the players' eyes were any indication, Ty knew the problems ahead would be worse than anything since his parents' car crash.

CHAPTER FORTY-FOUR

THE BENGALS TOOK THE opening kickoff back for a touchdown. The crowd grew angry, hurling insults and, in some cases, cups of beer over the walls and out onto the field. When the Jets got the ball, their offense sputtered. They couldn't run, and Pennington, the Jets quarterback, didn't have either of his top two wide receivers to throw to. The Bengals blitzed on almost every third-down play, rushing linebackers and even safeties in at the quarterback along with the four defensive linemen.

The Jets defense did their part, though, and kept the Bengals pinned down into their own territory. A fumbled punt gave the Jets good field position, and two plays later, Thomas Jones ran in for a twelve-yard touchdown. At halftime Ty followed Thane into the locker room after the rest of the players. Inside, the players sat on the stools in front of their lockers watching the coaches as they drew up plays on grease boards and yelled at certain players to exert more effort or be smarter. The serious mood infected Ty, and he didn't even try to talk to Thane. He just sat and watched and listened.

In the second half, the Jets started out well, moving the ball on the ground and driving down for a field goal. Ty looked at the clock—only 2:54 left in the third quarter. He wished the rest of the time could speed by with no more scoring. If the Jets won 10–7, everyone would be happy. The Jets would have the victory they wanted without Thane, and Uncle Gus would win his bet. Although Uncle Gus put money on the Bengals, he could win the bet even if the Jets won the game. The point spread of eight meant that as long as the Jets didn't win by nine or more points, Uncle Gus and everyone who bet on the Bengals would be happy.

If the Jets scored another touchdown and went up by ten, the Jets would win, but Uncle Gus would lose all his money. Ty began to root for the Bengals, quietly shifting his hips and shoulders with the Bengals quarterback, willing him to avoid getting tackled and to keep the ball down on the other end of the field.

He must have rooted too hard, because the Bengals scored a touchdown of their own in the beginning of the fourth quarter with a long pass to Chad Johnson.

The Bengals now had a 14–10 lead, so Ty could safely root, all-out, for the Jets. A Jets touchdown would give them a 17–14 lead and Uncle Gus would still win his bet. The Jets offense crossed the fifty-yard line, but Pennington got sacked on third and five and they elected to punt the ball. The Bengals took the ball from the ten all the way to the Jets' thirty-five, tried a fifty-two-yard field goal, and missed.

The Jets ran three plays without any success and had to punt again. By the time they got the ball back, only 3:46 remained, not much time without a good passing game that could gain yardage in big chunks. The Jets started to run with some success, gaining five, six, seven yards a play, but the chunks weren't big enough. The clock wound down. They kept going, driving across midfield and into Bengals territory. With thirteen seconds left, Jones got tackled on the three-yard line. The Jets offense scrambled to the line of scrimmage, setting up and snapping the ball so Pennington could throw it down into the ground and stop the clock. One second remained. One play for the Jets to win.

Ty stood with Thane and the rest of the team and coaches, crunched together in one corner of the bench area. Ty watched the coaches talking into their headsets, nodding to each other before they turned their attention to the field. Ty watched Pennington cover the ear holes of his helmet so he could hear the play being radioed in. He knelt down in the huddle and emerged a few seconds later with the rest of his team, jogging to the line.

The Bengals defense crowded the line, jab stepping and moving in and out of the gaps between the defensive linemen, who were hunkered down in four-point stances, heads low, like hogs ready to root out grubs. The ball was snapped. The clock ran down. Like everyone else on the Jets sideline, Ty held his breath.

CHAPTER FORTY-FIVE

PENNINGTON FAKED A HANDOFF to Jones and rolled out on a bootleg. He pump faked the pass, then dove across the goal line himself, taking a crushing hit from the Bengals safety that sent the ball flying out of his hands, but not before it crossed the line. The ref signaled touchdown. The Jets won by three and Uncle Gus won his bet. The crowd went wild and so did Ty and Thane, jumping up and down, roaring, and hugging each other until Thane hobbled sideways on his bad knee.

The festive air in the locker room smelled of sweat and hot showers. The players' banter bubbled up over the sounds of reporters' questions and the hissing water, and even though Thane hadn't played in the game, his voice, too, rode the back of a nearly constant giggle. Players hugged and slapped hands and snapped each other with their towels. They chortled and laughed and made plans to get together afterward, some at nightclubs, some at one another's houses to watch the Sunday night game.

Several players asked Thane to join them, but he answered that he had plans with Ty. Ty felt a little guilty but mostly proud and thankful that his brother wanted to spend time with him. As they walked through the underground tunnel, Ty noticed the crowd of other players' families and friends waiting for them behind a velvet rope. Most wore green-and-white Jets gear, but almost as many dressed in leather jackets, new shoes, designer jeans or slacks, and silk or cotton shirts with collars.

One woman stood alone with a short leather jacket, snug jeans, and high-heeled boots. Her dark hair spilled around the padded shoulders of her jacket, and when she saw Thane, she blushed and looked down.

"Hang on a minute," Thane said to Ty, planting him in his spot and walking over to the girl.

Thane put his hands on her shoulders. She looked up at him, and he kissed her lightly, saying something that made her laugh before giving her a cheerful good-bye and returning to Ty. Inside the Escalade, Ty couldn't help asking who she was.

"Ah, this girl," Thane said. "Her name is Deena. She's okay. I gave her my tickets."

"She's awesome," Ty said.

Thane glanced at him with half a smile and said, "Yeah, she's pretty. Nice, too. That's the most important thing."

The truck rolled up out of the stadium and into a special lane the police had blocked off so that the players and coaches could get to the highway without waiting for traffic.

"Didn't you want to do something with her?" Ty said. "You didn't even introduce me."

"I will," Thane said, gently massaging his knee. "One day. I like to take things slow."

"Before you bring her into the family," Ty said.

Thane waved to the last of the policemen and pulled out onto the interstate before he said, "That's right. You gotta be an all-star to be in this family."

"Dad used to say that," Ty said.

Thane drove without saying anything for a little while, then said, "I know. I figure some of the things he said to me, I'd keep saying them to you. Tradition and all that."

Ty nodded.

"You don't mind, right?" Thane asked.

"I like it," Ty said.

"Where do you want to eat?" Thane asked. "I'm starved."

"Subway?"

"Subway?" Thane said. "I got a gold card. We can go anywhere in the world and you want Subway?"

"Chicken Bacon Ranch," Ty said. "Toasted. Nothing better."

"Barelli's?"

"That's different," Ty said. "You can't forget where you came from either."

"True."

Thane pulled off at the next exit and drove down the strip of fast-food stores and shopping centers until they found a Subway. Thane ate three sandwiches. Ty got two bags of BBQ chips to go along with his meal. They sat in the back corner and, still, nearly a dozen people came up to Thane, asking him to sign their Subway napkins. One guy had two kids younger than Ty, and he asked if it was okay to take a picture. Thane just smiled and nodded and did whatever people asked. And whenever he signed an autograph, he advised each person to get Ty's signature as well.

"Then when he's in the NFL, you can say you've got us both," Thane said. Some of the people smiled funny at him, said thanks, and walked away. Several, though, really did ask Ty to sign their napkins, too, and it made him blush.

The sky had faded to dark gray by the time they walked out of the Subway. They'd climbed into the big black truck and pulled out onto the street, heading for the mall and a movie, when flashing lights began to bounce around the inside of the cab. Thane checked his mirror.

"You've got to be kidding," he said, talking to himself as he pulled over to the curb. "I was, like, two miles over the speed limit."

Ty spun around and saw the dark Crown Vic, whose lights flashed on and off from inside the grille along with the steady beat of its high-beam headlights going on and off. Ty shielded his eyes and saw one dark shape get out while another stayed in the front seat of the car. The man who walked up to Thane's window wore a suit that flapped in the breeze. He tapped on the window, and when Thane rolled it down, he flipped open his wallet and flashed a badge with an FBI identification card.

"Tiger Lewis?" the man said, examining the inside of the truck and making quick eye contact with Ty.

"Yes."

"I'm Special Agent Kline. Would you mind coming with me?" the agent said.

"For what?" Thane asked.

"We need to talk with you, Tiger," the agent said with a somber look. "And I don't think this is a good place to do it. You can park your truck in that lot over there and get in with us."

"What, I'm not in trouble or anything, right?" Thane said with a laugh of disbelief.

The agent stared at Ty for a moment, then focused his attention on Thane and said, "I'd have to say that right now, Tiger, yes, you are in trouble. A lot of trouble."

"What about my brother?" Thane asked.

"You can bring him," the agent said, glancing at Ty. "I think you'll want to. He's right in the middle of this thing."

CHAPTER FORTY-SIX

THANE PULLED INTO THE shopping center and parked in an empty spot. The dark Crown Vic pulled in behind them, blocking them in as if to keep Thane from making a break for it.

"What the heck is this?" Thane asked, turning to Ty as he shut down the truck.

Ty couldn't speak. His throat felt too tight. His head spun. He shrugged, making a small unintelligible sound.

Thane shook his head, huffed, and got out. Ty followed him. Agent Kline opened the back door for them on his side of the car. Thane waved Ty in first. As he slid across the seat, he became instantly aware of the size of the man in the front seat. He'd not only moved his seat all the way back but reclined it halfway in order to accommodate his incredible bulk. Ty blinked at the long, wavy hair and the shaggy black beard.

"Mike?" he said without thinking.

Mike slung his arm over the back of the seat and swung halfway around. With a grim face he offered Ty a curt nod before turning back to face the front and somehow managing to fold his arms across his chest. Ty wedged himself behind Mike's seat. Thane got in, followed by Agent Kline.

Agent Kline turned around and said, "Tiger, this is Agent Kemblowski. Your brother knows him already."

Thane shot Ty a look, wrinkling his face and holding up his hands in a way that asked a question.

"He works in the bar we clean," Ty said. "That's all."

"He's an undercover agent," Agent Kline said, slipping the car into gear and pulling out onto the road. "We're both with the Organized Crime Task Force."

"How does this have anything to do with me? Us?" Thane asked.

"Let's talk when we get there," Agent Kline said.

"Where?" Thane asked. "Should I have my lawyer?"

"Not unless you want us to arrest you," Agent Kline said.

Thane closed his mouth and clenched his hands, staring straight ahead, his face lined with concern. After a while he patted Ty's leg and whispered to him not to worry, but his voice sounded strained.

Agent Kline drove through an industrial area, then turned down a broken road and pulled into a vacant lot surrounded by a ten-foot chain-link fence with a scroll of barbed wire, surveillance cameras every twenty feet, warning signs, and electric gates. Inside, a single electric pole shed a white cone of light down on a large construction trailer. They pulled through the gates. Broken bits of concrete and stone crunched beneath the tires.

"What is this place?" Thane asked, his body rigid.

"It's a place where no one will see you talking to two federal agents," Kline said, pulling up in front of the trailer. "That wouldn't be a good idea."

"Kind of unhealthy to be working with us when you're dealing with these people," Mike said. "Best to keep things on the low."

Agent Kline got out. Mike followed, and so did Thane and Ty. The trailer's metal steps groaned under Mike's weight. Inside were several desks cluttered with phones and papers. In the back, a small conference table shared the room with an easel that supported a large corkboard. Photographs of various men covered the board, with index cards beneath bearing their names. Colored yarn, red or white, connected many of them. In the bottom right corner, Ty's school picture jumped out at him. Next to it, Thane smiled back from the photo used in the Jets media guide.

Ty followed the yarn with his eyes, up the board, from him and Thane, to Uncle Gus, to Lucy, up through two other men Ty thought he'd seen playing poker at Ludi's Meats, and finally, to "Big Al" D'Amico at the very top.

Ty gulped, trying to keep his Chicken Bacon Ranch down. He sat next to Thane, facing the two agents. Mike wore a dark blue windbreaker and, beneath it, a Rutgers Athletic Department T-shirt. Nothing suggested his status as an FBI agent, except the knowing look in his eye that Ty had recognized but until now hadn't had a name for.

Agent Kline brushed a lock of straight blond hair from his face and stared at them with dark blue eyes. He straightened his striped tie, looked at Mike, folded his hands across the notepad in front of him, and said, "We're pretty sure that, dollar for dollar, today was the biggest sports betting scam since the White Sox threw the World Series."

"What the heck are you guys talking about?" Thane asked, laying his hands flat on the table.

"We're talking about you mysteriously bailing out of today's game when there was an eight-point spread," Mike said in his low rumble, pointing a finger at Thane. "We're talking about the D'Amico family and its members clearing over *seven hundred thousand dollars* in bets. Your own uncle made fifteen thousand."

Thane shook his head, a look of disbelief plastered across his face. He turned slowly toward Ty, frowned, and said, "Is this what your fantasy football questions were all about?"

Ty's eyes filled with tears.

Thane slammed his palm down on the table, filling the trailer with the echo of its crash.

"Is it?" he shouted.

CHAPTER FORTY-SEVEN

TY COULD ONLY NOD his head, biting his cheek to stop the tears.

"I didn't mean to," he said. "Honest. I didn't want Uncle Gus to keep asking you for money and I thought he'd stop if I helped him. They said it was for *fantasy* football."

"But when you met with Big Al D'Amico Friday night," Mike said, glaring at Ty, "you knew it wasn't fantasy football then."

"Friday night?" Thane asked, arching his eyebrows.

Mike nodded. "We followed him and your uncle to one of D'Amico's hangouts. On Saturday, all the money started to move to Cincinnati. They basically flooded the betting market, knowing that you weren't going to play. Meanwhile, the average Joe was out there thinking you were and betting on the Jets to win by more than eight."

"We'd like to know if your knee is really hurt," Agent Kline said.

"You think I faked it?" Thane asked, squinting at the agent and shaking his head in disbelief.

"He didn't know anything!" Ty said, jumping to his feet. "They filled a tube of bloody gunk with what they took out of his knee right before the game! You can ask the team doctor. I saw it!"

"Settle down, kid," Agent Kline said.

"I don't care what you do to me!" Ty shouted. "You leave him alone!"

"No one's doing anything to anyone," Agent Kline said. "We just want your help. That's why we're talking to you like this instead of serving you with a warrant. If you faked it, that's different. Giving this kind of information to those people is a crime, yeah, but not like actually faking an injury to affect the outcome of a game."

"I would never do that," Thane said.

"And you'd testify to that?" Agent Kline asked.

"Of course."

"And you'll help us in this investigation?"

"I'll help," Thane said.

They all looked at each other for a minute before Thane asked, "What's this going to do to our aunt and uncle?"

"And Charlotte?" Ty said.

Mike shrugged and said, "We don't need your uncle's help. He's going to go down with the rest of them."

Thane looked down at the table for a moment, then said, "I don't want that."

"Hey, Tiger," Mike said, "no offense, but this guy's been a grade A jerk to your little brother here."

Thane looked at Ty. Ty shrugged.

"My aunt and uncle took Ty into their home," Thane said. "It's what our parents asked for in their will."

Mike stroked his beard.

"They took Ty in when we didn't have anyone else," Thane said.

Mike looked at Agent Kline.

"Even if you forget about Uncle Gus," Thane said, "what about Aunt Virginia and our cousin Charlotte? What happens to them if he goes to jail? I'm not turning my back on them. If you want me, they're part of the deal. You have to help Gus, too."

"I don't know if you really get what's going on here," Agent Kline said. "Sure, we'd like to help you out. You seem like a good guy, like you got caught up in this without really knowing. But guess what? That's what they all say."

"It's true!" Ty said.

"But when the jury hears everyone singing the

same song, D'Amico, Lucy, your uncle," Agent Kline said, "then your story gets lost in all theirs and you all look like one big pack of liars. Trust me on this."

"You need to forget about your uncle," Mike said. "You need to save your own skin."

"So, are you with us?" Agent Kline asked. "What do you say?"

"I say," Thane said, "I need to talk to my lawyer."

Mike threw his hands up. Kline huffed and rolled his eyes.

"I can't promise you this deal's gonna be here tomorrow," Agent Kline said.

"Then it's not much of a deal," Thane said, standing up. "I take it we can go?"

"For now," Kline said.

Thane put his arm on Ty's shoulder.

"So, you'll take us back to my truck?" Thane asked.

"Of course," Kline said, getting up and jangling his keys.

"Tiger," Mike said, tearing a scrap of paper off of Kline's notepad and jotting down a number, "take this. It's my cell phone. Have your lawyer call me. He'll know. You come out on the wrong side of things with this and you can forget your football career. That'll be over."

CHAPTER FORTY-EIGHT

THE AGENTS DROPPED THEM off at Thane's truck and peeled away quick enough to make their tires yip like small dogs. Ty climbed into the truck. Thane sat staring straight ahead, then gripped the steering wheel and rested his head on it.

"I'm sor—"

"Don't say it," Thane said, holding up a hand for Ty to stop. "They got you. They get people a lot older and more street smart than you, so don't start blaming yourself."

"They're talking about your *career*," Ty said.

"You didn't know," Thane said.

"Are you sure about Uncle Gus?" Ty asked.

"No, but Aunt Virginia? That's Dad's sister," Thane said. "Charlotte's our cousin. Like it or not, Uncle Gus

244

is family, and no one knows better than you and me how important family is."

"Because ours is gone?"

"Because it's still here," Thane said. "You and me. Nothing more important than that, right? Nothing we wouldn't do for each other."

Thane started the truck and pulled out of the lot.

"Where are we going?"

"Morty's."

"Don't you want to call him?"

"Something like this you don't talk about on the phone," Thane said, heading for the highway.

Morty lived on the Upper East Side of Manhattan, in a high-rise that looked out over Central Park. He greeted them in a pair of slippers and red-and-white striped pajamas. They followed him through the marble entry-way and into the library, with its smell of books and leather furniture. Instead of going to his desk over by the big window, Morty sat down on the couch and flicked off the Sunday night game.

"Sorry you caught me like this," Morty said, pinching the sleeve of his pajamas. "If the game gets boring, I usually end up asleep on the couch, and I hate waking up with my clothes on. What's so urgent?"

As Thane told the story, Morty's face grew tighter and tighter, wrinkling his brow and pinching his lips until he looked ten years older.

"Why do you look like that?" Thane asked when he'd finished. "I didn't do anything wrong."

"Innocence never got in the way of ruining a public figure before," Morty said.

"Public figure?" Ty asked.

"Someone in the news," Morty said, "on the sports page. Someone people talk about. Just your connection to this is enough to ruin everything."

"What do I do?" Thane asked.

Morty put his hand over his mouth and massaged his cheeks.

"We give up your uncle, make you a CI, a cooperating informant, and this whole thing can come off like you're working *with* the FBI from the start," Morty said. "You could come out of it like a hero."

"I'm worried about my aunt," Thane said. "He's her husband. She doesn't even work."

"And Charlotte," Ty said.

"I'm worried about you," Morty said. "That's my job. No offense to them, but it's too bad."

Thane thought about that for a minute, then shook his head and said, "No, we've got to at least try. If it comes down to it, we can give them Gus and I can help out my aunt, but I want you to try to cut a deal to save him, too."

"We're not in a great position to bargain here," Morty said.

"That's what you do, right?" Thane said. "Bargain."

"Thane—"

"No, Morty," Thane said, holding up a hand. "I mean it. They took my brother into their home. They're not the greatest people in the world, but they treated him like family the best they know how. How can I not do the same thing? You've got to try to save them, too."

"What if I try and I lose the deal you've got right now? You'd throw everything you've worked for away to save that . . . that . . ."

"Dork," Ty said.

"That dork," Morty said.

Thane just looked at him with his mouth set and the muscles in his jaw rippling.

Morty nodded and sighed. "Well, if there's a deal to be had, you know I'll get it. Let me have that agent's number."

"You going to call him now?" Thane asked.

"I work well at night, even in pajamas."

Morty slipped on a pair of reading glasses, read the number, and dialed. He demanded a face-to-face meeting with Mike and Kline, saying that the alternative was for him to talk to a friend of his who wrote a sports column for the *Post*. He smiled as he wrote down the name and address of the place they'd meet and then hung up the phone.

"They hate the media worse than professional athletes do," Morty said.

"I don't hate the media," Thane said.

"Give it time," Morty said. "Anyway, let me try to get this worked out."

"What should I do?" Thane asked.

"Don't you have to get Ty back?" Morty asked. "You need to act normal. We don't want to attract attention, especially from your uncle. Not yet."

Thane put his arm on Ty's shoulder and started to leave.

"Wait," Ty said, turning to Morty. "I've got an idea."

"What do you think this is, the science fair or something?" Morty asked.

"What if we give up Uncle Gus but save him, too?" Ty asked. "He could testify, but then they could let him go."

"Problem there is the mob," Morty said. "Uncle Gus is in on this deal. He's their partner. If Thane testifies, that's one thing. He's just an innocent bystander. He's not betraying anyone. But these people have a pretty rigid code. If your uncle sells these people down the river? They'll kill him."

Ty swallowed, then said, "Witness protection. What about that?"

Morty looked at Thane, who asked, "Why not?"

CHAPTER FORTY-NINE

UNCLE GUS BARELY NOTICED when Ty walked through the door. He sat in his old chair, but the old TV had been replaced by a fifty-inch plasma with surround sound that resonated through the house. In the middle of the smoke Uncle Gus sucked on a big cigar, its orange tip burning brightly. He raised his beer can to Ty.

"Football hero!" he shouted. "That's what you are. Did you see it? The Jets looked like crap. Come here, you. Come sit down and take a look at this picture. This is what happens when you grab the brass ring! The first taste of success!"

Uncle Gus turned his eyes to the screen and belched.

"Where's Aunt Virginia?" Ty asked.

"Holed up with the girl," Uncle Gus said, his face

showing annoyance, "reading books. The two of them."

Uncle Gus turned his attention back to Ty. He squinted and said, "You're into that book thing, too, aren't you?"

"The teachers are always telling us to read," Ty said.

"It's not that *manly* if you ask me," Uncle Gus said, his cheeks collapsing in on themselves as he sucked the cigar. "Beer. Cigars. Football games on a big-screen TV. That's a man's work. Where you going?"

Ty pretended to yawn. "I've got school tomorrow, and practice."

"Well, you earned it for once," Uncle Gus said, reaching into the tub beside his chair and cracking open a fresh can of beer.

Ty fled to his space in the laundry room and pulled the chain to turn on the light. He tipped his bed down and took a battered library copy of *Harry Potter* out of his pillowcase book bag. More than anytime before, he needed to lose himself in the world of his book, but this time, he couldn't. In his mind, wizards turned into mob bosses, and warlocks became hit men and bookies.

When he heard a scratching sound at the door by the woodpile, Ty felt a chill. He could imagine Big Al's people—having somehow found out that they'd spoken with the FBI—coming to take care of him. The tapping persisted, and Ty snapped off the light, then crept past the door to the small window, where he peered out into the night. In the glow of the stars, he saw Charlotte.

"What are you doing?" he said in a hiss, twisting the lock and yanking open the door.

"I went out through my window," she said. "I didn't want him to know we were talking."

"What's the matter?" Ty said. "You scared the heck out of me."

Charlotte peered at him with her big eyes and said, "I want to know what's going on."

"What do you mean?"

"He went crazy during that game," Charlotte said. "When the Jets went ahead by ten, his face turned purple and he was cursing you and Tiger up one side and down the other. I mean, he went nuts. Then the Bengals scored and he jumped around screaming that you're the greatest. He picked me up and swung me around."

"Gosh," Ty said.

"Then he goes to the mall and comes home with a new TV," she said. "An *expensive* new TV, and he starts talking about going to Bermuda on a vacation. I don't even know where Bermuda is. Has he finally lost his mind, or is there a reason?"

Ty looked out into the dark kitchen and at the glow of the doorway that led to the living room. He pulled Charlotte deeper into the shadows, and in a whisper he said, "Charlotte, if I tell you, will you promise not to tell anyone? Not even your mom? Because you can't."

Charlotte nodded.

Ty leaned close so that he could speak directly into her ear, and he told her everything. When he got to the part about Uncle Gus and the FBI and jail, Charlotte gasped.

"You can't let them," she said, gripping him by the shoulders, her face rumpled and ready to spill tears.

"Thane's doing everything he can," Ty said. "We've got a plan, and Morty is going to try to cut a deal with the FBI."

"Morty?" Charlotte said. "He hates my father."

"Morty is Thane's agent," Ty said. "He'll do everything he can. Thane will be crazy mad if Morty doesn't get it done."

"Why would he?" Charlotte asked.

Ty shook his head. "It's just him. It's because we're family and Uncle Gus is our aunt's husband. He's your father, too."

"Some job he does," Charlotte said.

"I know it's bad sometimes," Ty said. "But it could be worse. He doesn't hit you or your mom or anything like that. He's just . . ."

"A jug head," Charlotte said.

"Kind of," Ty said. "But don't worry."

"Why? You're not?"

"A little," Ty said, "but when Thane gets it in his head to do something, it usually gets done."

Charlotte hugged him and patted the back of his head.

"Thank you, Ty," she said. "You're the best cousin anyone could ever have. You're really more like my brother."

Charlotte turned and let herself out the side door, quietly closing it. Ty turned the lock and peered out the window toward the front, glad not to see a pair of mysterious headlights heading down the dirt drive carrying two ugly men looking for him.

He lay back down on his bed and closed his eyes.

Sometime in the early morning hours, the cigar smoke began to subside and Ty finally fell asleep.

Ty had trouble keeping his eyes open during classes. Twice in math he yawned, and his teacher said the third time would earn him detention. At practice, Ty watched the road for Thane's Escalade or the FBI's Crown Vic. The thought of a black Cadillac pulling up and rolling down its rear window to sprout a gun barrel wouldn't stop popping into his mind either. It didn't surprise him that he dropped every other pass, but Coach V didn't understand, and he wasn't happy.

"Lewis!" he shouted after Ty let one bounce off his chest in the end zone. "Get your head out of the clouds! Are you kidding me? We've got Brookfield in five days!"

After practice, Coach V called Ty into his office and told him to close the door.

"You like me okay, right, Lewis?" Coach V asked, taking off his sunglasses.

"Sure, Coach," Ty said.

"You chumped out that jerk West and I came to your defense," Coach V said.

Ty nodded.

"I like coaching this team, Lewis," he said.

Ty nodded again but shifted his feet, his skin feeling tight.

"But I won't be if we don't win this game against Brookfield," Coach V said, staring down at his open hands as if he'd dropped something.

"You're a winning coach," Ty said.

"You'd think that would count for something," Coach V replied, "but not always. Sometimes it's not enough. I've been here five years now, and every year we do pretty good. But it's about Brookfield. They've got the program everyone else wants to have, from the middle school team all the way up to the varsity. When I came here, they told me my job was to beat Brookfield. That's what the athletic director and everyone else wanted. They told me I had five years, and I didn't really think they were completely serious."

"But they are?" Ty asked.

Coach V nodded. "Apparently, yes. So, I'm sorry I was chewing you out nonstop today, but you're my guy, Lewis. Without you, I don't win this game, and I like this place. So, when I see you dropping balls like that . . . well, I wanted you to know what's going on. I like you, Lewis. Forget about football; I like you a lot. You're a good kid, and if I'm lucky enough to have my own kids one day, well, I hope they turn out like you."

Ty's cheeks began burning and he looked down at his shoes.

"That's all," Coach V said.

Ty thanked him—for what, he didn't know—and returned to his locker.

When Ty walked out of the locker room, he expected Uncle Gus but saw Thane waiting instead. Ty jogged up to the Escalade.

"Get in," Thane said.

"Where's Uncle Gus?" Ty asked.

"Don't worry. I've got it covered," Thane said. "Just get in and I'll tell you the plan."

CHAPTER FIFTY

TY LISTENED TO THE plan but couldn't think of anything to say once he'd heard it.

Finally he said, "I'm scared."

Thane turned down the road between the old abandoned factories, toward the place where the FBI kept their trailer.

"I am, too," he said.

"You are?" Ty asked, blinking his eyes and staring at Thane, expecting him to laugh at his own joke.

"Anyone who does something dangerous to help other people is either scared or stupid," Thane said. "Heck, I'm scared all the time. Scared I'll get hurt. Scared I won't succeed. I'm scared every time the phone rings."

"The phone?" Ty said.

Thane pulled up to the gate and honked his horn,

then looked at Ty. "Like when the police called me about Mom and Dad. That was the worst thing that ever happened to me."

"Well," Ty said quietly, "*that* can't happen again."

Thane's eyes glistened, and for a moment it looked like he might cry. He reached over and messed up Ty's hair.

"As long as you're okay, it can't," he said.

The gate rumbled open and they drove into the broken lot.

"That's Uncle Gus's truck," Ty said, noticing it for the first time between the trailer and several dark sedans.

"Yup," Thane said.

They got out and Ty followed his brother up into the trailer. This time several people in shirts and ties occupied the desks, either talking on the phone or working at their computers. One of the men pointed toward the back of the trailer. In the conference room, Uncle Gus sat staring at the corkboard in disbelief. Charlotte sat there, too, her hands in her lap and looking off into space, a million miles away.

The man sitting beside Agent Kline wasn't Mike but another agent in a blue suit and, around the edges of his balding head, dark hair that matched his wiry black mustache.

When Uncle Gus saw them, he stood up and wrung his hands. "Tiger, I didn't mean any of this. You've got to believe me."

"I understand, Uncle Gus," Thane said. "We'll get it worked out."

"I can't do this," Uncle Gus said, looking around. "These people, you just don't do this to them."

"Like I told you, Mr. Slatz," Kline said, "if we do this without you, you're looking at ten to fifteen years for racketeering."

"I didn't do anything but win some money," Uncle Gus said, whining.

"We've got you on tape talking about Tiger's injury and how you knew he wasn't going to play," Kline said. "There isn't a jury in the world that won't put you away."

Uncle Gus's face sagged. He nodded his head.

"Thane and Ty," Kline said, turning his attention to them, "this is my boss, Special Agent in Charge Dominic Mueller."

Mueller stood up and shook hands with them both before they all sat down again.

"So, I just do the same thing I did before?" Uncle Gus said. "That's all?"

"It's pretty simple," Kline said. "Tiger will practice all week. If he does that, he won't be on injury list. You tell Big Al's crew that even though he practiced, the knee is bothering him again and he's not going to play, same as last week. They all bet against the Jets, but then he really does go out and play. Hopefully they win, or at least beat the point spread, and the mob gets burned pretty good."

"If they find out, they'll kill me," Uncle Gus said, his face draining of color.

"That's what we're counting on," Mueller said.

Uncle Gus made a choking sound.

"With the evidence we gave the judge from this weekend," Kline said, "we've got fresh wiretaps and bugs all over the place. If D'Amico gives the order to take you out, we can get them on a murder conspiracy."

"We get that and the whole bunch of them will go away for a very long time," Mueller said.

"We'll have protection assigned to you," Kline said. "As soon as this goes down, we'll get you and your family away from here. You'll be completely safe. When the trial happens, we'll bring you in and back out in a day. No one will know where."

"Away where?" Uncle Gus asked.

Kline shrugged. "Spokane, Fargo, Odessa, any- place you like. Someplace small and out of the way. You'll be safe. We've never had a problem with some- one in the Federal Witness Protection Program. We'll find you a job. The house and essentials are taken care of."

"Isn't Odessa in the desert?" Uncle Gus said.

"We'll give you a list of choices," Agent Kline said.

"Don't have much choice, do I?" Uncle Gus said.

"Not if you don't like wearing one of those orange jumpsuits," Agent Kline said with a frown.

"I heard Spokane's not so bad," Uncle Gus said.

That's when Charlotte began to cry.

CHAPTER FIFTY-ONE

AT NIGHT, TY HAD trouble sleeping. At work, he went through the motions of cleaning. Uncle Gus didn't say much of anything to him, and Charlotte was in a total fog. During the day, he had a hard time keeping his eyes open in school and his hands around the ball during practice.

By Friday, all Coach V could talk about was the enormous Brookfield defensive line, the incredible speed of their secondary, and their nearly unstoppable running back. The coach seemed almost resigned that they'd lose on Saturday, but Ty had much bigger things on his mind, and as much as he liked Coach V, he just couldn't make himself care.

When Thane arrived Friday night, Uncle Gus ran out to the truck and grabbed hold of Thane's open window. Ty climbed into the passenger seat.

"So, you're feeling good?" Uncle Gus asked Thane.

"Real good," Thane said.

"Then this should really work, right?" Uncle Gus asked.

"We're all scared, Uncle Gus," Thane said.

"Oh, I'm not," Uncle Gus said. "It's the FBI. They know what they're doing. They do this all the time, right?"

"Okay, well," Thane said, "I better get going. Hey, since you're here, how about putting these up inside your accounts, or in their windows? Help spread the word."

Thane took a stack of posters from the backseat and handed them through the window.

"They made up these posters for an autograph signing I'm doing at the mall this Saturday and the next for the Boys and Girls Club," Thane said.

"Are they paying you?" Uncle Gus asked.

Thane looked at him for a moment with half a smile, as if expecting a laugh, then shook his head. "It's for charity, Uncle Gus."

"Oh. Right," Uncle Gus said. "I was just thinking about everything else we've got going on. You know."

"We're supposed to just act like normal, right?" Thane said.

"Yeah, that's right," Uncle Gus said. "And you're ready to play for sure?"

"But we're not telling *them* that," Thane said.

"No, I know," Uncle Gus said. "We tell them you're dropping out, that your knee flared up again same as last week and you're done. Without you, they're going to feel pretty safe betting on Miami. So, you sure you two are okay? You don't want any company?"

"Everything the same, remember?" Thane said.

Uncle Gus nodded and removed his hands from the window. "Right, right. Okay. You two have fun."

As they drove away, Ty said, "'You two have fun'? What's up with that?"

"He's just nervous," Thane said. "How about Barelli's?"

"Sure."

"Just 'sure'? You lost your appetite?" Thane asked.

"Until this is over, I think I did," Ty said. "Plus, I don't trust Uncle Gus."

"What do you mean?"

"He's not so nice," Ty said.

"I never said he was," Thane said.

"Believe it or not, he puts his best foot forward for you," Ty said. "I think he's up to something."

"Like?"

"I don't know," Ty said. "But I'm gonna find out."

CHAPTER FIFTY-TWO

AFTER DINNER AND A movie, Thane dropped Ty off in front of the house.

"We didn't even talk about your game tomorrow," Thane said. "It's the big Brookfield rivalry, right?"

"Well, you know," Ty said with a wave of his hand, "with all this."

Thane nodded but said, "A football game is a big thing."

"But I thought—"

"I know, you've got all this stuff on your mind, but think about it. You only play how many games?"

"Ten."

"Ten games," Thane said. "You work year-round getting ready for the season, lifting weights, running till you're sick, then comes training camp, all those practices, day after day in the heat. Then you only get ten or sixteen or whatever chances to really play the game. It's something special. You can't let anything get between you and that."

"Even Big Al?" Ty said.

"Remember the car accident?" Thane asked, his voice taking on a somber tone. "I had a game the day after the funeral. I didn't care about the game, about football. I didn't care if I ever played again. But I had ninety other guys and twelve coaches counting on me. No one asked me to play. They would have been okay if I didn't. But this game, it's the ultimate team game. You need everyone to win it."

"Coach V said if we lose, he's gone," Ty said.

"Fired for one game?"

Ty shrugged. "Brookfield is the best. They gave him five years to beat them."

Thane nodded as if that made complete sense. "See? And they need you, right?"

"I guess."

"A great player doesn't perform his best when everything's good," Thane said. "He performs his best when it isn't."

"I never said I was great," Ty said in a mutter.

Thane lifted his chin and looked him in the eye. "Hey, look at me. You're a Lewis."

Ty set his mouth and nodded that he understood.

"Three o'clock, right?" Thane said. "I'm coming

straight over after the charity signing. I should be able to just make it for kickoff."

Ty thanked his brother, got out, and watched him go. When he walked into the house, Uncle Gus directed him right back outside, loaded him into his truck, and drove straight to Ludi's Meats. Three times on the way, Uncle Gus reached into his coat pocket and removed a roll of Tums. With a shaky hand, he popped the stomach medicine into his mouth straight from the roll, crunching it down and swallowing and leaving little powdery crumbs in his mustache. Even through the cigarettes, Ty could smell the sour odor of Uncle Gus's nervous perspiration. When they arrived, Uncle Gus tripped on the curb and stumbled again on their way up the narrow stairs.

It looked like the same set of characters in the same smoky cloud to Ty, only this time, Lucy sat facing the door, right next to Big Al. Lucy threw down his cards and jumped up, his red scar glowing like the picture in Ty's science book of the spot on Jupiter.

"There he is," Lucy said warmly, opening his arms.

They all turned around, grunting their welcomes. Big Al leaned back in his chair and tugged a wad of money from his pants pocket. He counted out ten hundred dollar bills in a wheezy voice and waved them at Lucy.

"This is for the kid," Big Al said, speaking without removing the stub of a fat cigar from the corner of his mouth. "For college or something."

Lucy took the money and circled the table, holding the money out for Ty. Ty folded the crisp stack of bills and tucked them into his pants without saying anything.

"So?" Big Al said in a bellow. "Where are we this week? The Jets are favored by one. How's your brother?"

Big Al's eyes sparkled at Ty with the ferocity of a snake preparing to strike. Ty opened his mouth to speak, but nothing came out. He gulped. Uncle Gus nudged him and cleared his own throat with a squeaky sound.

"Not going to play," Uncle Gus said.

Big Al narrowed his eyes and removed the pulverized tip of the cigar from his mouth, pointing it at Uncle Gus but nodding his head at Ty. "I want to hear *him* say it."

Uncle Gus nudged him again and Ty found his voice.

"He's not going to play," Ty said.

"Practiced all week but not going to play?" Big Al said with a glimmer in his eye that Ty couldn't read.

Ty nodded. "That's what he said."

"Was he limping?"

"Yeah," Ty said. "The knee's all swelled up. It does that, poof, all of a sudden."

"You saw it?" Big Al asked.

"Like a grapefruit," Ty said.

"That's a pretty safe bet then, isn't it?" Big Al asked.

Everyone nodded and grunted and grinned. Lucy patted Ty on the back, nearly knocking him down.

Inside the truck, Uncle Gus held his hand out to Ty.

"What?" Ty asked.

"The money," Uncle Gus said. "This is my deal, not yours."

"He gave it to me," Ty said.

Uncle Gus just stared at him and snapped the fingers of his outstretched hand until Ty removed the ten hundreds from his pocket and handed them over. Uncle Gus stuck them in his shirt pocket and began to whistle.

"That went well," he said, pulling away from the curb. "You looked like you were ready to wet your pants in there."

Ty flashed him an evil look and opened his mouth to say something but thought better of it.

"You could learn from me, boy," Uncle Gus said, glancing over at him. "A lot of people see dirty toilets. I see never-ending business. You get it?"

Ty shook his head.

"No, you got no business savvy," Uncle Gus said. "Just like your brother with that agent of his. Watch and learn."

Instead of turning for home, Uncle Gus got on the highway and headed south. Ty fell asleep, only to wake as they pulled into the brightly lit circular drive of an Atlantic City casino. The clock on the dashboard said one-thirty. Uncle Gus reached under the seat and removed a brown bag, peeking in at its contents and poking the tip of his tongue out from beneath the bristles of his mustache. He hopped out and gave the valet some money, telling him he needed only five minutes and to leave the truck right where it was.

"Watch and learn if you like," Uncle Gus said, slamming his door closed.

Ty scrambled out and took off after his uncle.

CHAPTER FIFTY-THREE

UNCLE GUS WADDLED THROUGH the towering doors of glass and gold. Ty followed him through a maze of colors and chrome, ringing slot machines, rattling roulette tables, and the call of dealers playing twenty-one. Uncle Gus disappeared through an archway. Ty followed and found a bank of televisions plastered across a huge wall. People sat with drinks at small tables, watching everything from horse racing to volleyball. Uncle Gus hurried to a long counter beneath a sign that said, SPORTS BOOK.

Ty crept up behind him and watched as he removed several stacks of bills from his paper bag, added the money he'd taken from Ty, and pushed it across the counter to a young woman in a red blazer.

"All on the Jets this Sunday," Uncle Gus said,

slapping his palm on the countertop.

The woman raised her eyebrows and counted out the money, thirteen thousand dollars. The woman punched some numbers into her keyboard, then handed him a receipt. Uncle Gus turned, winked at Ty, and motioned for him to follow as he hustled back out to the truck. He fired up the engine and pulled back out onto the road, then interrupted his grin long enough to whistle a little tune that Ty recognized as "Yankee Doodle Dandy."

When Uncle Gus roused him the next morning, Ty barely remembered getting home. Although tiny webs of blood vessels crept from the corners of Uncle Gus's eyes, his call to get up suggested plenty of energy. Ty groaned and looked at his clock, then sprang up out of bed. They usually started their Saturday morning rounds at eight and finished by two. His game today against Brookfield was at three. The clock read 8:37.

He tipped his mattress against the wall, threw on his sneakers, scooped up the laundry bag that held his uniform, and dashed into the kitchen.

"We've got to go," Ty said.

"Am I the only one with an alarm clock in this house?" Uncle Gus asked, sipping from a mug of coffee. Aunt Virginia sat in her robe reading the paper and shaking her head.

"My game is at three, Uncle Gus," Ty said. "I have to be there at two for warm-ups."

Uncle Gus looked at his watch, pursed his lips, and shook his head.

"I don't know," he said. "We're gonna have to clean fast."

Charlotte gave Ty a sympathetic look. She hopped up from the table and rinsed her cereal bowl in the sink. "I'm ready."

"Off we go," Uncle Gus said, taking his coffee with him and heading for the front door.

Ty cleaned like a tornado, finishing his work and diving in to help Charlotte with hers. The only thing Uncle Gus did to help was hang up the posters Thane had given him, proudly announcing to passersby that Tiger was his nephew. On Saturdays, they usually cleaned Lucy's last, and that's where they found themselves at ten after one. Since Lucy's was only twenty minutes from Halpern Middle School, if they finished in half an hour, Ty could still get to the game on time.

He rushed in the back door with his supplies and charged right past the kitchen.

"Hey, kid," Mike said, sticking his head out into the hall and waving his hand for Ty to come back.

The outside metal door behind Mike banged open, bringing with it Uncle Gus carrying his last poster and Charlotte toting the vacuum. Mike opened his mouth to speak, then closed it.

"I'm gonna be late," Ty said, backing through the swinging door to the men's room, banging his mop handle against the wall. "I got a game."

Mike opened his mouth again to say something, but the door swung closed and Ty darted into the men's room, spilling ammonia into the bucket and filling it with water before splashing it onto the floor with his mop and getting to work. The filth no longer made him ill, and even the stench no longer seemed like a shocking offense but rather a small annoyance. He flushed the toilet and turned at the sound of the door opening.

Mike held a finger to his lips, signaling Ty to keep quiet. He held the backpack Ty had seen before in his hand. Mike moved closer and in a low voice said, "Something's up."

Ty felt a chill.

"Like what?" he asked in a whisper. "Something with Thane?"

"I don't know," Mike said, removing some kind of wand from his pack along with an electronic box and a set of headphones all connected by black wires, "but Lucy banged his crowbar on the bar about twenty minutes ago and he's been in his office ever since. Your uncle just went in there with him."

On cue, the thin sound of Lucy's shouting floated out of the vent inside the stall. Mike's eyes shot toward the stall, then returned to Ty.

"If you put your ear to the vent, you can hear in there," Ty said.

"How do you think I know so much about what's

going on?" Mike said, raising the electronic equipment that Ty now recognized as a microphone and recording device.

Ty scurried into the stall and knelt down by the vent. Mike wedged himself halfway in, slipped the headphones over his ears, and poked the microphone over Ty's shoulder, clicking on the recorder.

"Sit down," Lucy said in a voice pleasant but laced with tension.

"Everything okay?" Uncle Gus asked. "Look, I got one of these posters for you."

"Real nice," Lucy said. "A charity thing, huh? Your nephew. This thing is right now, huh?"

"Next Saturday, too," Uncle Gus said, his voice trailing off. "I thought it'd look good on the wall, you know, to make the connection with Tiger maybe showing up here sometimes. It's a good action shot."

"Yeah, it is," Lucy said. "So, everything else okay?"

"Sure," Uncle Gus said.

"You must be feeling pretty good about the game tomorrow, huh?" Lucy said.

"Sure," Uncle Gus said, forcing a laugh. "It's good for all of us. Nothing like a sure thing."

The silence lasted so long that Ty wondered if they'd left the office, but just as he turned to Mike with a questioning look, Lucy slammed his crowbar down on what sounded like his desk. Ty jumped.

"Sure thing?" Lucy said, raising his voice to a roar.

"A sure thing going the other way! You didn't think we'd find out? You put thirteen thousand dollars on the Jets down in Atlantic City and you didn't think I'd find out about that?"

Uncle Gus began to whimper. "Lucy, I can explain."

"Don't you even *talk* to me!" Lucy said, screaming and smashing something with the crowbar. "I'll tell you what's going to happen *now*. That nephew of yours? You think he's going to play in that game tomorrow? You think you can cross *us*? Well, that ain't gonna happen."

"Lucy, what are you going to do?"

"I'm going to save you *and* me from a swim in the Passaic River with concrete shoes," Lucy said. "That kid plays tomorrow and Big Al's gonna blame me, too, because I'm the one that brought you to him. Now, you're gonna wait right here until I get back. Don't you even move from that chair."

"You're not going to use that?" Uncle Gus said with a moan.

"You think he's got a bad knee now?" Lucy said. "Wait till I get through with his knee."

Ty had barely digested Lucy's words before the door to the bar owner's office swung open and slammed shut again.

CHAPTER FIFTY-FOUR

TY STRUGGLED TO GET past Mike, pushing the giant to make room in the stall's doorway.

"Easy," Mike said, holding the recorder and microphone up in the air to protect them from Ty as he wormed his way out of the stall. "You'll break it."

Ty squeezed past him and dashed for the bathroom door, only to be yanked into the air. Mike had him by the back of his shirt.

"Wait," Mike said in his low, rumbling voice. "I got to stow this stuff."

Mike scooped up the backpack and stuck his listening equipment inside. "Settle down."

"He's going after my brother!" Ty said.

"You can't go anywhere without me," Mike said, zipping up the pack. "I don't want any of the regulars out there to see you and me shooting out of here. I'll walk out, calmly, and after a minute, you follow me to the back. Don't worry. We'll find him first."

"But Lucy's already on his way there," Ty said, pushing at Mike again, but without success.

"On his way where?" Mike asked.

"The mall," Ty said. "Thane's doing a signing. It's on the poster. We've got to get him."

"You telling me he knows where Tiger is?" Mike said.

Ty nodded and Mike spun around, yanking open the door, grabbing Ty by the arm and dashing through the back of the bar, down the hallway and out the back. They hopped into Mike's rusty Jeep but had to stop when Charlotte appeared and stood with her hands held out, blocking their path. Mike leaned on the horn, and Ty shouted to get out of the way, but she stood her ground.

Ty hopped out and yanked open the back door. "Come on!"

Charlotte circled the Jeep and jumped in, slamming her door at the same time Ty shut his own. Mike's tires shrieked, and off they went like a rocket.

Mike took one hand off the wheel, flipped open his phone, and hit a speed dial.

"Kline?" he said. "It's me. We got a problem. I think we're blown and Lucy's on his way to the mall to do I don't know what to Tiger Lewis."

Mike paused to listen.

"Forget the case," Mike said, raising his voice. "Get the locals over there. Everyone you can. Find Tiger and grab Lucy."

There was another pause as Mike darted between cars and ran through a yellow light blaring his horn. Mike glanced at Ty and asked, "Do you know where in the mall?"

"No," Ty said.

"No," Mike said into the phone. "Just get them there."

Mike ended the call and handed Ty the phone. "Call mall security and see if you can find out where your brother is."

"Should I tell them someone's coming to hurt my brother?" Ty asked.

"It's worth a try," Mike said, rounding a corner so hard that they nearly rolled over.

Ty got an answering machine, pushed zero for customer service, and got put on hold. Mike shot onto the highway, and when traffic clogged up, he passed everyone on the right, driving full speed down the breakdown lane all the way to the next exit. Ty could see the mall before they even got off. The Jeep fishtailed as Mike wound his way through the maze of the parking lot. Ty searched the rows of cars and the other traffic for a sign of Lucy. Mike came to an abrupt halt right in front of the doors, and they jumped out into the throng of people just as someone from customer service got on the line.

Ty asked if the man knew where the Tiger Lewis signing was, and the man put him on hold again. They ran up the escalators, searching frantically. There were four levels of shops. Ty ran for the center of the mall thinking it the most likely place for a charity event to be. Charlotte nearly kept his pace, but by the time they reached the center, Mike had dropped back. Ty spun in circles, his eyes aching for some sign of his brother. He looked up at the next two levels and down through the open center at the food court below. Mobs of people washed past him, with no idea about the crazy mobster ready to destroy his brother's career.

He couldn't stand there. He had to move, so he took off running. He'd cover every square inch of the place if he had to. Halfway down one section, he heard Charlotte screeching his name. He spun, eyes darting this way and that, looking for Thane, thinking she must have seen him. He didn't see a thing, though, and he shot a frustrated look back at Charlotte's pale face. She stabbed her finger at two people walking his way, a young boy with his father. Ty wrinkled his brow and threw his hands up, exasperated.

"What?" he shouted, jogging back toward his cousin.

By this time, Charlotte had caught up to the father and son, and she grabbed the older man by the sleeve.

Ty arrived, noticing now that the boy had a football under one arm.

"Did you get Tiger to sign that?" Charlotte asked the man, breathless.

"Anybody can," the man said. "It costs twenty bucks, but it goes to charity."

"Where?" Charlotte asked.

"Right here," the boy said.

"But where?" Charlotte asked, her voice pitched to a frenzy. "Where here?"

"By the movie theater," the father said, pointing. "At the other end of the mall. The top floor."

Ty took off on a sprint. He streaked past Mike, shouting that Thane was by the movie theater. Halfway there, he saw an escalator to the top floor thick with people. Over by a department store, he saw a set of stairs. He headed for them instead, shooting straight up to the fourth floor, taking the steps three at a time.

There were only a few people on the top level except for at the far end of the mall. Ty saw a crowd gathered in front of the movie theaters, where Tiger was signing autographs. A second escalator ran up the open space in the middle of the mall from the floor below, ending directly in front of the theaters. Two couples got off at the top, and halfway down, on his way up, Ty recognized Lucy. He held his right hand stiff to his side. Just below his knee Ty could make out the clawed hook of the crowbar.

Ty shouted, but the crowd burst into applause and no one seemed to hear. The signing must be over. Thane would be a perfect target for Lucy as he made his way through the crowd.

Ty's lungs burned from running and his side ached, but the sight of Lucy riding calmly up the escalator ignited something deep inside him. He found his burst of speed, raced down the last stretch, rounded the corner, and reached the head of the escalator just as Lucy stepped off.

CHAPTER FIFTY-FIVE

USING THE SAME TECHNIQUE Thane had shown him on the blocking dummy, the same technique he'd stalked Calvin West with, Ty coiled and sprang at Lucy, both hands striking him dead center in the chest at the same time. With one foot on the escalator and one foot in midair, Lucy tipped back, grasping empty space with one hand and instinctively swinging the crowbar with the other. The weapon whistled past Ty's head. It struck the opposite handrail; a shriek tore free from Lucy's throat as he fell.

Lucy's head hit the escalator steps with a thump just as his feet circled over him in a horrible cartwheel. As his crumpled legs hit the stairs, his battered head came up, arms still flailing, only to go back down again. Tumbling this way, Lucy bumped and banged his way to the very bottom, coming to rest in a broken heap at the base of the escalator just as Mike staggered up between two policemen with their guns drawn.

The FBI agents wanted statements from everyone immediately. Nearly two hours passed before Ty climbed into Thane's Escalade and remembered he had a football game.

"You've been pretty busy," Thane said, navigating the SUV out of the parking lot at the federal office building.

Ty's muscles felt drained of energy, but the idea of Coach V getting canned fired him up.

"My stuff's in Uncle Gus's truck," Ty said. "It's at Lucy's."

Uncle Gus had been scooped up by some other agents at Lucy's and was still inside the federal office building, answering questions.

"Does he lock it?" Thane asked.

"It's in the back with the cleaning stuff," Ty said. "The lock's broken."

Thane stepped on the gas to make a traffic light. They retrieved Ty's uniform and raced to the game. As they rode down the street to the football field, the scoreboard came into view. Halpern was down 21–10 with only six minutes to go. Sickness exploded inside Ty's stomach like a cherry bomb.

"You'll have to hurry," Thane said, pulling up onto the curb. Ty grabbed his equipment.

"I'll tell the coach so he knows you're coming," Thane shouted as Ty sprinted across the blacktop behind the school, toward the locker room.

Ty tried to slow his frantic breathing and quell the tremble in his fingers as he laced, buckled, and yanked on his gear. Finally, he burst through the locker room door, heading for the field, throwing on his helmet and snapping his chinstrap into place. Parents filled the small set of bleachers on the Halpern side of the field, but the Brookfield crowd spilled out of their bleachers, blanketing the hillside and surrounding the field like an invading army.

Two of the six minutes in the final quarter had already expired. Halpern had the ball, but the scoreboard said they faced a fourth down with eight yards to go. Coach V saw Ty and called a time-out.

Ty arrived, breathless, at the little group of players surrounding Coach V. Thane stood near the bench, giving him a thumbs-up.

"You ready?" Coach V asked, looking from Poyer, the quarterback, to Ty.

They both nodded yes.

"We can still do this," the coach said, then called a midrange pass play that would send Ty on a twelve-yard hook. "Get the first down and then we'll go for the end zone."

Ty went to the huddle, accepting hand slaps from several teammates before listening to the play and lining up. When the center hiked the ball, Ty shot forward, startling the cornerback with the distance he covered in a split second. He ran by at full speed, the cornerback turning his hips and starting to sprint, desperate to keep up.

At twelve yards, Ty planted a foot and hooked back toward the quarterback. Poyer zipped the ball before Ty even spun. There it was! With the speed of a frog's tongue, Ty snatched the ball from the air but got hit from both sides.

He felt the ball come loose as he crumpled to the ground.

CHAPTER FIFTY-SIX

TY HUNG ON. THEY had the first down they needed. As promised, Coach V sent Ty for a long bomb on the very next play. He beat the defenders to the goal line by nearly ten yards, catching Poyer's pass and closing the gap to 21–16. The team swarmed Ty, and the Halpern sideline erupted with joy. They kicked the extra point to make it 21–17, but they'd need another touchdown to win. When Ty returned to the sideline, Thane collared him and bent down to whisper in his ear.

"They won't let you get that deep again," Thane said. "I watched their coach grab the free safety when he came off the field. They'll put him deep over the top of you every play, all the way to the goal line if they have to. The long bomb won't work."

"How about a comeback pass?" Ty asked.

Thane nodded. "That's what I was thinking."

Ty grinned at him and went in search of Poyer.

The Halpern defense struggled to stop Brookfield. When they finally held, it was within field-goal range. Brookfield made the kick, widening their lead to 24–17. Halpern's running back returned the kickoff to the forty, but as Ty jogged out onto the field, less than a minute remained.

Coach V called for Ty to run an out-cut, sprinting twelve yards up the field and breaking for the sideline. If he could catch the ball and get out-of-bounds, they'd close in on the goal line and stop the clock, too. It worked! The next time they tried the same thing, but there were three players guarding Ty now—one lined up inside, one outside, and one over the top to protect the end zone.

On third down, a Brookfield linebacker got through on a blitz and sacked Poyer. Fourth down would be the team's last chance. Ty ran to the sideline.

"The comeback," he said to Coach V. "Send me deep. Poyer knows what to do."

A comeback pass would send Ty into and then back out of the end zone, with Poyer throwing the pass shorter than the last bomb he'd thrown.

Coach V jabbed his finger at the clock on the scoreboard. Only fifteen seconds remained.

"We're out of time-outs!" the coach said. "You don't get into the end zone, we can't stop the clock and it's over."

"I'll get in," Ty said.

Coach V sucked his lower lip under his teeth but nodded and sent him back out onto the field, then signaled the play to Poyer. Ty lined up, eyeing the trio of defenders waiting for him. At the snap, he rocketed forward, sprinting for the end zone. The free safety took off for the goal line with a fifteen-yard head start. Ty left the two closer defenders in his dust, but the safety had turned and was waiting for him on the other side of the goal line, expecting the deep ball. Ty took two steps into the end zone, then suddenly stopped and darted back, the ball already in the air and coming down somewhere around the two-yard line.

Ty caught it, but the two lagging defenders caught up and hit him instantly, one high, one low. He twisted and pumped his legs. The safety, recovered from the deep fake, burst out of the end zone and launched himself at Ty's head. Ty ducked, never stopping his feet, driving through the low tackler, dragging the high tackler with him another foot, then falling to the ground, the ball in his hands like a precious egg, his arms outstretched.

Touchdown.

In the riot of the celebration, Ty had the wind knocked out of him by his own teammates. Just five seconds remained. The score was 24–23. Coach V waved Ty and Poyer to the sideline, removed his glasses so they could see his eyes, and hung his arms around their shoulders.

"We can't kick the extra point. We've got to go for two," he said. "One play. Three yards. A fade route to Ty. They're going to be looking for it. Poyer, you've got to throw it high into the corner.

"Ty, you've got to outjump them all. This is it."

The two of them ran to the huddle. As the offense lined up on the ball, the crowd of parents and spectators from both sides rose to their feet, roaring so loud it made the quarterback's voice difficult to hear. Four defenders surrounded Ty this time. He looked over to the sideline at his brother. Thumbs-up.

The center snapped the ball. Ty dodged the first defender but took a shot from the second. He stumbled, breaking inside, head faking the third before he broke back out for the corner of the end zone. The fourth defender was waiting for him. Ty got to the corner, turned, and leaped with all his might. The ball was already arriving in a blur, a forest of fingertips groping for it.

Ty stretched with every ounce of energy he had. It wasn't enough. A Brookfield defender tipped the ball, knocking it off its path before Ty could get his hands on it. The ball flipped end over end, wobbling and falling toward the ground.

Ty watched it as he fell, knowing it was out of reach. Everything slowed and he heard a whisper from the past.

CHAPTER FIFTY-SEVEN

"YOU DON'T EVER QUIT," *Thane said, flicking off the TV with the remote so that the two of them sat in the total dark with only the ghost of the TV screen anchoring them to their place in the universe. "That's the rule. You never give up."*

"But the game was over," Ty said, quiet in the emptiness.

"It's not over until it's over," Thane said, speaking slowly, the way he did when he wanted Ty to remember. "You want to be a champion, you have to think that way, in everything you do. You never stop. You let yourself start to think that way, then the one time you could pull out a win because of some freak luck, you're not ready for it. Maybe it's only once in a lifetime, but that's one win you'd never have, and who knows what that one win could do."

* * *

It was over.

The ground came up fast, gravity snapping him into place, pounding his ribs and lungs with a powerful stroke, but his eyes stayed with the ball. He couldn't quit. So, when the ball bounced off a defender's shoulder pad and screwed sideways, his hands went with it. The ball dropped again, but his fingers stayed between it and the grass. Through the jolt of pain and shock, his fingers tightened and held on and he lifted his hands—with the ball—into the air. The referee looked down at Ty with an open mouth. He stood straight, lengthening the black-and-white stripes of his sleeves skyward to signal the score.

Two points.

Halpern 25, Brookfield 24.

They raised him up off the grass, his teammates. Then Coach V and his own brother each took a leg and raised him even higher. They paraded him around the field, a hero, as the Brookfield fans dispersed like a broken wave.

CHAPTER FIFTY-EIGHT

THE HAPPY BANTER OF victory between Thane and Ty didn't end until they pulled up to Uncle Gus's later that day. A dark sedan with two serious-looking men in suits stood guarding the entrance to the drive. Inside the house, Aunt Virginia emerged from her bedroom with a suitcase in each hand, struggling under their weight. Uncle Gus pulled back the curtain every few seconds to peek out the picture window.

"You think those guys out there could stop a delivery truck?" he asked. "'Cause Big Al owns a truck line, you know."

"You're fine," Agent Kline said, checking his watch. "We've got you all on a six-thirty flight to Atlanta. The drive to Jacksonville is about five hours from there, but that'll be best. They'll take some evasive action out on the open highway. They're pretty thorough."

Mike walked in from the kitchen, carrying the stack of three square plastic milk cartons containing Ty's worldly belongings.

"You got another suitcase for the kid's things?" he asked Aunt Virginia.

Ty felt his jaw go slack. His skin prickled with panic. He felt as though he were suddenly peering over the edge of a cliff. He couldn't see what waited beyond the edge, but he could sense the vast emptiness of it. Whatever waited out there, he knew it didn't include his new football team, being on the sideline with the Jets, and Friday evenings out with his big brother.

Aunt Virginia frowned and shook her head. "I could double up a couple trash bags. That'd hold it all pretty good."

"Where am I going?" Ty said.

Both agents, Aunt Virginia, and Uncle Gus stared at him.

"We're not gonna just leave you," Uncle Gus said. "No matter how much you eat."

Ty couldn't bring himself to look at Thane. He could feel him, standing there, rigid, beside him. His older brother's silence felt like a stranglehold on Ty's throat.

"It's time to tuck your uncle away someplace safe," Agent Kline said.

"Do you think one of Lucy's guys still might try to hurt Thane so he can't play?" Ty asked the agent.

"I *would* have thought that," Agent Kline said, "except Big Al heard about Lucy and he must have put two and two together. We heard him on the wire-tap betting the same amount of money he had on the Dolphins back on the Jets. So his money is safe."

"Won't they be mad at Thane?"

"Thane didn't do anything to them," Mike said, looking up as he dumped Ty's things into the doubled-up plastic garbage bags. "He never cut a deal with anyone. Trust me—he's as safe as the NFL comissioner."

"Okay, let's get it going," Agent Kline said as Mike knotted the ends of the garbage bags, slinging them over his shoulder like a bizarre, oversized Santa.

Uncle Gus checked the window before hefting his own enormous suitcase and making for the door. Charlotte appeared from her room, wearing her school backpack, a pink plastic suitcase in one hand, and her iPod in the other. When her eyes met Ty's, he thought he saw a flicker of sadness.

Ty felt Thane's hand on his shoulder, but then Agent Kline tugged on his arm and Thane's hand fell away. Outside, they loaded their things into the Crown Vic's spacious trunk. Uncle Gus slid into the car and gripped the headrest of the seat in front of him. Aunt Virginia climbed in and rested her head in her hands. Charlotte went in last, closed the door, and rolled down the window so she could peer up at him.

"You can sit between us in the front," Agent Kline said to Ty. "It'll be a little tight, but the airport's not that far."

It was all happening too fast. Ty needed to catch

his breath, but there was Mike's enormous paw on his other shoulder, leading him toward the car. And there was Thane, staring with his mouth hanging open, blinking in the late daylight, raising his hand in a feeble wave of good-bye.

CHAPTER FIFTY-NINE

"WAIT," THANE SAID, RAISING his voice loud enough so that Mike spun his big, hairy head around and stopped tugging Ty. "Why does he have to go?"

"Your brother?" Agent Kline asked.

"Yeah," Thane said.

The agent shrugged. "This is his family, right?"

"So am I," Thane said.

Ty saw movement in the open car window, Charlotte nodding her head, before he stared up at his brother.

"They're his guardians, right?" Mike said, raising his hands, palms up.

Uncle Gus leaned across his wife and daughter to address them through the open window. "Let's not miss this flight."

"Let me take Ty," Thane said, blurting out the words.

Uncle Gus's mouth popped open beneath his thick

gray mustache. His mouth turned down at the corners; then he worked a finger into his ear and said, "I guess. Why not?"

"We can take care of the paperwork later," Thane said to the agents.

Ty's head swam. Morty's words from draft day echoed through the back of his mind like a war drum.

"I can tell by the way he looks at you that if you asked, there's nothing he wouldn't give you, but don't. You gotta live your own life."

"What about *your* life?" Ty asked.

Thane gave him a funny look and his smile went crooked. "Yeah. So? You're in it. I got room."

Ty moved closer to his brother and whispered up into his ear. "What about Charlotte?"

"She can come," Thane said. "I doubt they'll let her, but she's okay with me. Go ahead. Ask."

Ty motioned to Charlotte, and she leaned outside the window. Into her ear he asked, "Do you want to come, too? He said it's okay with him, and I'd like it, too."

Charlotte beamed up at him but shook her head. She pulled him close, clutching the back of his neck and hugging him tight until his face felt hot.

"Thank you," she said, kissing his cheek. "I gotta go with them. You gotta stick with your family, right?"

She let Ty go and he smiled and winked at her, then said good-bye to his aunt and uncle, shaking their hands and thanking them for taking care of him. Mike shook Ty's hand, too. As the big agent climbed in, the car's frame dipped toward the ground. He closed the door and they drove off. As the car disappeared into the deep weeds, Thane put an arm around Ty and pulled him close.

Thane sighed, then looked down at him for a moment before he said in a serious tone, "I'm glad you said yes."

"Why wouldn't I?"

Thane shrugged. "You know, a mom and a dad, kind of. A sister. It was more of a family than just you and me. I'm not gonna make you brush your teeth or do your homework or give you chores or any of that. I just can't do that parental stuff."

"You don't have to," Ty said. "I got great teeth."

Thane smiled and said, "Yeah. Runs in the family."

"You think I can still go to Halpern somehow?" Ty asked, looking back down the empty drive after the sound of the Crown Vic accelerating out on the road.

"Sure," Thane said. "We'll work it out. I'll hire a limo or something."

"You don't have to do that," Ty said, looking up.

"Why? You need to start getting used to that stuff anyway," Thane said. "After what I saw today? Won't be long, you're a first-round pick yourself."

"You think?" Ty asked.

"I don't think it," Thane said, leading him toward the Escalade. "I know it. Football hero, that's you."